HE SAVED MY BOY

AMANDA SHELLEY

Visit my website at
www.amandashelley.com

CONNECT WITH AMANDA SHELLEY

Want to be the first to know about upcoming sales and new releases? Make sure you sign up for my newsletter as well as connect with me on social media and your favorite retail store.

Website:
www.amandashelley.com
Newsletter:
https://geni.us/AmandaShelleyNL
Facebook:
https://www.facebook.com/authoramandashelley/
Instagram:
https://www.instagram.com/authoramandashelley/
Reader's Group:
https://www.facebook.com/groups/AmandasArmyofReaders/
Tik Tok:
https://www.tiktok.com/@authoramandashelley
Amazon:
https://www.amazon.com/author/amandashelley
Goodreads:

https://www.goodreads.com/author/show/19713563.Aman
da_Shelley
Book Bub:
https://www.bookbub.com/profile/amanda-shelley

He Saved My Boy

Davis is the first guy to catch my attention since... hell, I don't even know.

Instantly, he makes me think and feel things I've forgotten existed. It has been forever since I put my needs first, so I take the chance and let him light me up from the inside out.

Our night is the kind that will ruin me for all others.

But then I get the dreaded call.

I rush out without a second glance, knowing I'll likely never see him again.

My son will always come first—Always.

Imagine my surprise when Davis walks in, and I find he's the only one who can save my boy.

This cannot be happening—*I guess it's time to pull up my big girl panties and see what happens.*

Chapter 1
Davis

MY FEET SLAP THE PAVEMENT, and my strides lengthen as I head off Main Street down a side road leading me to Tilly's Place. It's been one hell of a week, and I'm glad I've finally taken my brother's advice to get out of Austin.

I've spent the better part of two years completing my final residency. As the tension drains from my body, I regrettably admit—Derek is right. I need to get away and relax for a night or two. Before I know it, I'll be packing up to return to Washington, and I'll have never seen anything about Austin but the walls of the hospital.

I wouldn't say Deacon, Texas, is a destination I ever imagined for myself. But it's close enough I can enjoy a weekend away, while still covering for my mentor if his wife goes into labor early this week. When one of the nurses told me about this place, I had no idea I'd be stepping into a freaking Hallmark movie. I swear everyone knows everyone in this town, and they are dying to know what a *young fella* like myself is doing here on a vacation from the big city. Or at least that's what the two ladies older than my grandma asked before I left the local café just now.

If my sister, Dani, saw this place, she would probably make me stop to record everything, just so she could use this little town for a setting in one of her books. She's a best-selling romance author and if I had a dollar for each time she got lost in her head with some plot or another, I'd be able to retire and live a life of luxury. But I digress. This little town is not my typical destination location, but it has gotten me out of Austin —and that's the point. I need this break.

I've finally hit my stride when my music unexpectedly cuts off, and my phone rings. Seeing my brother Derek's name flash across my screen, I take the call and continue my run. He knows time is limited, and he'll just have to work out with me if he wants to talk.

"What's up, D?" I ask between pants.

"Please tell me you're running and not in bed with someone right now." He may sound like he's trying to protest, but I can tell from the tone of his voice, he's grinning from ear to ear with that smart-ass remark—I mean, what are older brothers for?

Shaking my head, I chuckle into the phone. "Dude... I'd never pick up if that were the case. I may like to multi-task, but even I have limits. How's that beautiful wife of yours? She ready to drop you like a hot potato and admit I'm the better catch?" He knows I'm full of shit, but it's something I stupidly said when I first met Tessa, and now it's kinda expected. Don't get me wrong, his wife is perfect—for him. I'd never see her any other way—than as my sister.

From his huff through the phone, I can just picture him

rolling his eyes and shaking his head. Before he can come up with an unneeded response, I quickly add, "Don't worry, D, I'm not sure I could keep up with her midnight cravings. How are you holding out?"

"Oh, I'd say those cravings won't be more than a distant memory as she went into labor early this morning."

This stops me dead in my tracks. "Come again?"

She isn't due for another three weeks. Bracing my hands on my knees, I take in air. If something's wrong, I need to give him my full attention.

"Well, it seems your niece, Melody, is a lot like her momma and is ready to take the world by the horns. We weren't even at the hospital two hours, and she arrived."

Three weeks early is considered full term, but I still have to ask—my years of training clicking in. Though if something were wrong—I'm sure he would've led with that. "How are she and Tessa doing?"

"Both are doing well now that Tessa's figured out her back pain was actually contractions. We would've probably delivered at home if I hadn't insisted on her being seen by her doctor. Thank God we arrived early enough for her to get an epidural, or I may never be able to draw again in my life."

During my rotation through the ER, I saw firsthand the strength of a woman in labor, and I cringe at the memory. I've always known women have amazing strength, but that rotation put my theory to the test. As a graphic designer, Derek needs his hands, so I tease, "Please tell me you at least gave her your non-dominant hand?"

Seeing as everything is all right, I walk back to the bed and breakfast I'm staying at for the next few days. No sense in standing here on the street like a crazed person on the phone. It's a small town; it's only a matter of time before someone stops to check on me.

He lets out an exasperated sigh. "Davy... had to switch them out, or I'd never get the feeling back. I've never been more thankful for her saying yes to drugs in my life, than when she agreed to that epidural. She was like a changed woman—in a matter of minutes. I'm tellin' ya, brother—I've never felt so friggin' helpless in my life. Watching her experience pain and not be able to do anything for her was the worst feeling in the world."

"I get it, man. When I was on my ER rotation, I helped deliver a baby in the freaking waiting room, and I swear, that woman could bend steel with her grip when her contractions hit. I'm just glad Tess is okay. Have you told the rents yet?"

Derek lets out a loud chuckle. "It was Mom who helped me convince Tess to see the doctor in the first place. I swear... Dad must've driven like a bat out of hell with the pedal to the metal the entire way. They were in the waiting room by the time I texted them to say Melody had been born."

Chuckling into the phone, "You know nothing will come between Mom and her grandchildren." I can only imagine what that car ride was like.

"You'd think we were having her first by the way she's been fawning all over Melody—not that I'm complaining. But Dame's twins are almost four, and Jules is ten—not to mention,

Dani's been a mom for more than five years—it's not like she's a first-time grandma."

"But Melody is your first, D. Let Mom have her moment. I'm sure Dad is riding that high right along with her. I swear both of them have gone backward in age since Jules came into their lives."

Derek practically snorts his response, "No kidding. Look, man... Just think—by the time you get around to giving them grandkids, maybe they'll be in their twenties again."

"Hey now," I protest out of duty. But let's face it—my life for the past eight years has been nothing but work, school, clinicals, residencies, and very little sleep. Rinse and repeat.

Before I can say anything further, Derek cuts me off. "Look, man, don't take it personally. I love you—but we all know you've had your priorities in the right place. I was just saying Mom and Dad get more energy with each new grandkid. By the time you have some—they'll act younger than you are now." We both laugh at that theory. God knows what my parents will do if I ever settle down. Thank God my sister and two brothers have been the buffers for me in that department—providing all the grandkids to keep them out of my personal life. I'd never hear the end of it if I were an only child. I swear, my parents were born to be grandparents.

"Look, Davy, I gotta call Damien."

This stops me in my tracks again. "I... got the call before Dame?" I exaggerate with a huge smile, then proclaim, "Wow... that must mean I'm her favorite uncle."

"You're gonna have to fight Dame and Luke over that title,

Davy. I just wanted to prepare you for the cuteness when I spam you with pics. I know you won't be able to see her until you return to Seattle next month but know we're thinking of you."

"I miss you, D. Give Tess a hug for me and that baby a kiss. Tell the rents I said hello."

"Dani and Luke just arrived, so when you get home, you're gonna have to up your game if you want that role of favorite uncle," he teases. "Enjoy your getaway, and we'll video chat once we're home from the hospital."

"Will do, D. Love you."

"Love you more, Davy," he says just as the line goes dead.

Damn. I'm an uncle—again. Seeing my brothers and sister become parents has been a welcomed change to our family dynamics. Sometimes I wonder what it'd be like to find a partner in life like they have, to settle down and have a family. But then again—I do enjoy being single—with my long hours at the hospital, that's what fits my lifestyle the best.

To finish my run, I pick up my pace and continue up the road. After a few minutes at my full speed, I notice a woman running about two hundred yards ahead of me. As I close the gap behind her, I see her dart down my next turn to the right. Not wanting her to think I'm a creeper, I slow my pace and wait to see where her next turn is.

We keep pace for quite a while, and I'm surprised to see it's not far off from my regular stride. Damn, even from here, I can tell she's much shorter than I am, but she's got some legs on her. Not only are they fast but sexy as hell, poking out of her running shorts. They're long and tone from years of running.

When she makes the final turn down the driveway to Tilly's Place—the bed and breakfast that's also my destination, I can't help but chuckle.

Maybe I am a creeper. The way I've been admiring her backside for the last three quarters of a mile has me dying to know if the rest of her looks just as good as my view from the back. Eventually, she slows her pace to a walk, and I do the same. No sense in making this any more awkward.

I watch her raise her hands to rest on her head as she regulates her breathing, just as I hit the gravel behind her. Instantly, she turns with a startled expression, and I feel like a total jackass for not announcing my presence earlier. "I... Uh... didn't mean to startle you," I quickly explain. "I guess we're both staying here."

Shaking her head, she grins. "That's what I get for getting in the zone. I'm used to paying attention in the city, but I let my guard slip."

Fuck. Now I really feel like an asshat. "I tried to stay far enough back, so you wouldn't feel creeped out—but what were the odds of us both ending up at Tilly's?"

"It's fine," she quickly reassures me. Then she gasps, pointing to my shirt. "Wait... you're a Rainier Renegades fan?"

From the shocked expression on her face, I hesitate for how to proceed and for the first time in forever, I swear my heart stalls. "Uh... yeah."

When her face morphs into a grin from ear to ear, I instantly release the breath I didn't know I'd been holding. "So am I. You've gotta be a die-hard fan—sporting those colors in Texas."

"Trust me—I know." I grin as she has no clue how deep my loyalties lie. "Our loyalty to the Renegades runs in the family," I add flippantly because hell, my family had been a fan of the Renegades long before Dani even knew my brother-in-law, Luke, existed. But damn—I'll never forget the day he walked into our house.

"I take it you're from Washington?" she says in a distinctly non-Southern drawl.

"Yep—I grew up outside of Leavenworth. You?"

Reaching for her foot to stretch her quad, she shrugs. "I'm currently living in Seattle."

Interesting. I'm half-tempted to say I will be, too—but that'd probably make me sound like a soon-to-be stalker—so I skip to a safe topic. "I've always liked visiting Seattle."

As I start my post-run stretching, we both sit in casual silence. When she leans into a calf stretch further, I'd be a liar if I didn't admit my eyes linger on her much longer than they should. Damn. I was right about her. She's even more striking from the front. Her long, brown hair is pulled back in a tight ponytail. Wisps of hair have fallen out in the front to shape her beautiful face. Without a stitch of makeup—her light-blue eyes and long, dark lashes captivate me. They're a stark contrast to her golden-brown skin, and I suddenly find myself wanting to get lost in them for days.

When she glances my way and catches me staring, I quickly blurt out, "Are you in town long?"

Taking in a deep breath, she switches legs. "I'm..." She pauses, then straightens her shoulders as she looks me in the eye once again. "I'm staying here for the rest of the week."

Seeing as it's only Tuesday, I grin. "Well, I'm here for the next few nights, too. Are you here with your family?" I dart my eyes to her ring finger, and my body loosens when I find it ringless.

"I... I'm here to see family of sorts—but to answer the question you actually asked..." She blows a bit of hair from her face, then turns a smile my way. "I'm taking a much needed me-cation."

A light laugh escapes at her sudden relief. "Well, everyone needs to unwind a bit. I guess that's why I'm here, too," I admit, then realize I have to know her name. "I'm Davis, by the way."

I swear, her cheeks darken as she glances quickly away, then returns those sky-blue eyes on me at full force. "I'm Teagan. It's nice to meet you. Are you visiting family?"

"No—they're back in Washington. I'm flying solo on this trip—a me-cation—as you called it."

A flock of birds takes flight from the trees that line the back of the property, momentarily drawing Teagan's attention. As soon as they've flown off, I swear I hear a rumble from Teagan's stomach. She closes her eyes momentarily, then turns to me and straightens her spine, looking far more confident and gorgeous than before. "I'm starving and need some breakfast. Care to join me?"

I had a bagel at the coffee shop earlier, but if she's asking me to spend more time with her, I'll gladly eat again. "Sure."

She sighs heavily, then hops up from the ground. "Okay. I need to grab a shower. Want to meet back in the lobby in thirty minutes or so?"

And just like that—I'm picturing her in the shower.

Fuck, man—get it together. You just met this woman.

But who am I to pass up an opportunity to spend more time with her? Besides, I'm here to unwind; if it involves her—I could eagerly get on board with that.

"Sounds good," I say as I follow her into Tilly's.

Once inside, she points down the hall toward my room. "I'm over here..."

Rolling my eyes, I grin as I shake my head at just what a bitch fate can be. "Apparently, I'm destined to look like a stalker with you—because so am I." I point at my room just two doors down. Seriously, I have more game than this.

Teagan's lips purse as she tries to hold back a grin as she walks down the hall. When she gets to her door, she says, "Well, *stalker,* if it gets to be too creepy, I'll be sure to change rooms."

"I'm sure that won't be necessary," I assure her.

She looks me in the eye, which causes my heart to stall unexpectedly.

What the hell is that about?

Taking in a deep breath, she slowly exhales. "I guess I'll be the judge of that, won't I? But for now..." Her stoic expression turns playful as she pulls her lower lip into her teeth. "I think we're safe in public places..."

When her stomach grumbles again, she laughs as she opens her door. "See you in thirty." Then she winks saucily at me as she scoots into her room and shuts the door.

She fucking winked.

I'm not sure how long I stare at her door before a noise at

the end of the hall has me picking my jaw off the floor and hightailing it to my room. I have no idea what will happen at breakfast, but I know one thing for certain—Teagan will certainly keep me on my toes.

This me-cation may turn out to be exactly what I need.

Chapter 2
Teagan

THE MINUTE the door is shut, I let out a small "Whoop" and rush to the bathroom to take the fastest shower possible. I freaking asked that hunk of a man out.

Me—Teagan Frost. The woman who wouldn't even know what to do with said hunk if he walked up and gave her explicit directions. Actually asked a practical stranger to breakfast.

I guess my friend, Annie, was right. I still have some game left in me. My swagger may be as dusty as an ancient tomb, but it's still there. It's time I finally do something for me and take a chance on some fun. God knows after the hell I've gone through, I deserve it.

Besides—what's the worst that can happen?

I'm in a public place. I can ask for a room change or hell—I can stay with the Harringtons if things get that bad. I know I'm always welcome, but I need this me-cation. I catch my reflection in the bathroom mirror and stop to look myself in the eye.

"Get it together, Teagan. You've got this."

Besides, it's just breakfast, and I only have thirty minutes.

Why the hell did I say thirty minutes?

Ripping back the shower curtain, I turn on the water and sigh heavily.

I barely wait until it's warm before I strip off my clothes and take my usual rush of a shower. Flying through my shower routine, I force myself to focus on each task rather than the fact I'm meeting Davis. This works out great until I find myself standing in only my bra and underwear in front of a suitcase I've yet to unpack, stewing over what to wear.

Thankfully, I'm saved by the bell—so to say—or a phone in my case. When my best friend's name flashes across the screen, I scramble to answer. "How did you know I need you?"

"Uh... I have special powers?" Confusion is obvious in her voice. "Everything okay, T?"

"Other than the fact I'm meeting a guy in less than twenty minutes, and I have no idea what to wear—I'm just peachy," I grumble, digging frantically through my suitcase, then realize I'm being rude. "How are you?"

"Whoa... back up. I'm fine, but who are you meeting?"

"Davis. He's a guy I met after my run this morning. I... uh asked him to breakfast here at the B&B."

If I weren't in a hurry, I'd probably laugh at her sudden intake of air. "Wow. That's just wow... Okay... So, you said you need help?"

"What do I wear, Annie? I haven't been on a date in—God, let's not even go there. But for some reason, I got a wild hair up my ass... And the next thing I know, I asked him to breakfast... in thirty minutes!" I nearly screech that last part because the clock is ticking, and I'm still in my underwear.

"Did you pack a dress like I told you?"

Originally, I'd planned on wearing a pair of jean shorts and a loose tank today, but the moment I see the splash of royal blue peek out from under my pile of clothes, my decision is made. "Yes, Mom, I did. Thank you." As I reach for the sleeveless dress that hits just at my knees, I smile at my snarkiness. Usually, I am the one giving advice, so it's hard not to roll my eyes in this moment.

But like a true best friend, she doesn't miss a beat. "I told you that dress could come in handy. Not only is it cute, but it makes your eyes pop and accentuates your best assets."

Yes, it does. But my favorite part about this dress is that it's extremely forgiving about the parts I love to conceal—and it has pockets. Who doesn't love pockets?

"As much as it pains me to say," I tease. "You're right. I did need this." Putting her on speaker, I slip it over my head and return to the bathroom to quickly apply minimal makeup and wrangle my mane of hair.

"So... tell me about this Davis. What do we know about him?"

Shit. Not much. So, I preface with... "I just met him, but he's from Washington—a Rainier Renegades fan and grew up outside of Leavenworth. Apparently, we're both staying here for the next few days." I laugh at the memory of him worrying about being a stalker. Then I quickly tell her how we met, and she joins me in laughter when I explain we're even staying in the same hall.

When I finish, she's unusually quiet for a moment, so I break the silence, "What aren't you saying?" Clearly, she has something on her mind. This is Annie. I've known her since we were six. This girl's wheels are clearly spinning.

"Shouldn't I be asking that?" I can hear the smile in her voice. "But…" She trails off. "Since you made the first move—I gotta know… just how hot is this guy?"

Closing my eyes, I picture his thick, dark hair, square jaw, beautiful lips, and eyes I could get lost in. He fills out a pair of shorts and that Renegades shirt perfectly. He's well over six feet and has a presence about him I just can't describe. "Uh… hot doesn't even do him justice," I quietly admit.

"That's what I thought." I can hear a smirk forming on her face. "Look, I know you need to get going, but do you want me to call in an hour so you can fake an emergency, if necessary?"

I don't think I'll need it, but it's nice to have an out. "Sure —but if it goes directly to voicemail, know that I'm having a great time." When I realize I need my full concentration to quickly throw my hair into a braid, so I can avoid looking like a drowned rat, I admit, "Look, Annie, I gotta go. I'll talk to you in an hour. I have about five minutes to get downstairs, and I still need to do something with my hair."

"Okay, T. Have fun, and I'll check in soon."

As soon as I'm off the phone, I finish my hair, apply some Chapstick, grab my purse, and rush out the door with only minutes to spare.

Just as I step into the hall, I jump when I hear from behind me, "You really will think I'm a stalker if we keep this up."

Turning on a dime, I see Davis's lips quirk as if he's trying to hide a smile." Damn. Freshly showered Davis is a sight to see. His hair is stylishly tousled, and his aqua button-down shirt fits him like a glove. It accentuates his best features—in the best ways possible. My eyes drift from his muscular chest to his corded forearms on display under his rolled-up sleeves to his elbows. His untucked shirt hangs over his light-gray shorts as if they were made especially for him. His tan muscular legs look even better in these than when we first met.

Holy hell, how had I missed the rest of him?

When Davis clears his throat, I'm drawn out of my ogling.

Shoot. Has he said something?

Instead of staring at him like a loon, I respond to his first question, "It seems we have impeccable timing."

His lips spread into a playful grin as he nods. "It seems we do. You ready to eat?"

"Yep. I've heard great things about the breakfast here," I admit as I turn to walk down the hall.

By the time we get to the dining room, I'm surprised to see we practically have the room to ourselves. Then again, it is getting closer to lunch than breakfast. A woman at a table looking at some paperwork greets us with a friendly smile. "Mornin'. Help yourselves to some coffee, tea, or juice. Can I interest you in French toast and some eggs? I got some Georgia peaches in yesterday, and they are to die for."

"That sounds amazing," I admit as my stomach rumbles in anticipation, causing Davis to chortle, followed by a groan from me. I can't get any breaks with this guy.

The woman, being the professional she is, hops up from her seat and quickly says, "I'll be right out with your breakfast."

After pouring some iced tea for me, Davis grabs a coffee for himself. Then he gestures to a table out of the way—should more guests arrive. The moment we're settled, he asks, "Got any plans while you're in town on your me-cation?"

Of course, he asks when my mouth is full of tea. It takes me a moment to swallow, causing both of us to grin. "I've been here a few times, but I've never taken the time to be a tourist. I'd like to go on a riverboat tour."

"Really? Why's that?"

Where do I even begin? Shrugging, I do my best to explain, "I guess the thought of actually seeing a bayou lined with cypress trees seems fascinating. Besides, the tour guide also gives a bit of the town's history. While I'm here, I'll probably head back into town and check out the shops. What are your plans while you're here?"

Davis bites on his lower lip and rolls his eyes as his head slowly shakes. Holding a finger out to me, he digs his phone from his pocket. Quickly, he unlocks his phone and pulls something up, then a small laugh escapes as he pulls the phone close to his chest. "Before I tell you my plans, I want you to take note of the reservation I made days ago."

Immediately, I recognize the riverboat logo. But before I can say anything, he asks, "Is this the tour company you've booked?"

Trying to fight the corners of my lips from turning up, I nod and fight like hell to keep a straight face. "Yep. I booked it before I went for my run this morning."

Davis takes a drink from his coffee and smirks. "Look who's the stalker now?"

"I'm pretty sure that title still goes to you. But..." I draw out for effect. "If you play your cards right, maybe we can go together."

A dark brow lifts in challenge, as he leans back in his chair. "And just what would I have to do to play my cards right?"

My stomach literally flips as if the floor just dropped out from under me as his lips quirk and strong arms cross over his broad chest. When his arms flex, I swear my mouth dries and my tongue sticks to the roof of my mouth. Holy hell. Davis is hot.

What the hell is this man doing to me?

Trying to sound unaffected by his sudden smolder projecting my way, I straighten and clear my throat. "Well..." What are my conditions? "Let's start with breakfast. If we're not tired of each other by then, I'm open to going to the river with you."

"Okay—I think I can live with that. Just one condition..." *What on earth could his condition be?*

He must sense my hesitation because he suddenly leans forward and adds, "Don't worry—it's harmless. I just need to pick up something for my niece. I can't be in the running for favorite uncle if I don't get a gift to them before they get home from the hospital. I just found out she's arrived a few weeks early, so I haven't picked out anything yet."

Can ovaries explode? Because his eagerness to be this child's favorite uncle is both adorable and impressive.

"Uh, it would likely get to her faster if you found something online and shipped it."

He nods in agreement. "True..." Then he holds up a finger. "But any of my brothers or brother-in-law could just one-click.

Trust me—that's how I usually roll. But since I can't travel to see her in person, I need to bring out the big guns. Maybe I'll strike out, but it'll be worth looking. I could hit the mother lode and easily climb my way to the top of her long list of uncles."

Davis is adorable in his determination to be the best. "Just how many uncles are you competing with?"

"I'm the youngest of four. Derek—my oldest brother is the newest father. When my siblings spoused up—and popped out kids, it's been a fierce competition." He stops momentarily, his nose scrunches up unexpectedly, and his mouth twists to the side as if he's suddenly remembering something. "Damn, if we're talking about Damien's kids—I guess Vince is among my competitors, too."

Mentally, I tick off the list he just mentioned, trying to make sure I follow his logic. "Do you have all brothers? Or is there a sister mixed in there?"

"Just one—Dani. She's right behind Derek and before Damien. And before you say anything—Yes, we all have D names. It's became a family tradition now that my siblings are having kids, too."

Thankfully, I don't have to because we're interrupted with the arrival of our breakfast. Not only do the fluffy pieces of toast make my mouth water, but the sliced peaches smell divine.

As the friendly woman sets our plates in front of us, she smiles. Then, in that Southern tone I've come to enjoy as a visitor to Texas, she offers, "Here ya go. If you need anything else, I'm Tilly, and I'd be happy to get it for you."

After thanking Tilly, I can't help myself from tasting the

golden perfection in front of me. A moan escapes my mouth as I devour it. Before I know it, I've eaten an entire piece. Eventually, when I look up, I find Davis looking at me with a bemused expression.

"What?" I ask, suddenly feeling self-conscious.

Shaking his head as if he doesn't realize he had been staring, he shrugs. "It's nothing. Just got lost in thought, that's all."

Not sure if I should press the issue, I point to his plate with my fork. "You going to eat?"

Cutting off a chunk of toast, he quickly shoves it in his mouth with a goofy grin. When his eyes never leave mine, a sudden tremor zings down my spine and flips in my belly. This is something I haven't felt in years—well before meeting Davis. I'm not sure what to make of it.

Somehow, he must sense my reaction because he finishes chewing and says, "What do you say we hurry up and get out of here?"

In this moment, I can think of a million things I'd like to let myself do with him—if only we were alone. But I'm certain his words were meant to be innocent. Unlike the sudden left turn of my befuddled brain.

How long has it even been since I let myself think those thoughts—let alone act upon them?

When Davis just stares, waiting for a reaction, I answer both of our questions. "It's been way too long since I've been spontaneous and just went with things. Promise me one thing..."

Cocking his head to the side, he raises a brow. "And what's that?"

Shaking my head, I admit, "I tend to get stuck in my head. Promise me that we'll focus on fun and go with the flow today."

Davis's eyes crinkle in the corners as he nods. "I'm positive I can hold you to that."

Chapter 3
Davis

FOR A MOMENT, I'm not sure what Teagan will make me promise. I fear she might say I'll agree to spend the day with you—but only as a friend. And that would be a freaking crime. The more time I spend with her, the more I find I like her.

She's smart—not just book smart. She seems to know all kinds of random facts, which keeps me on my toes. But she's also witty and has a sense of humor that hits me square in the solar plexus. By the time we make it to the riverboat tour, both my stomach and cheeks ache from laughing so much.

The moment we pull into the parking lot, I feel as if I've just entered a time warp. Though the tour company has made it into the twenty-first century with its social media, the building itself appears as if it's been along this bayou for at least a hundred years. Sure, there's a fresh coat of paint, but it looks about the size of a home built back in the late 1800s.

As Teagan and I walk across the small dock to get to the boat house, I find myself placing a hand at the base of her back to guide her ahead of me. Normally, I'm not a touchy-feely kind of guy, however with her, I like the way this feels. I don't have time to contemplate my revelation because she suddenly stops and gasps.

Pointing to a spot in the river, she spits out, "Oh my God, did you see that?"

All I see is the ripple of water that obviously is from something big that has caused it. "No. What did I miss?"

"I'm not sure, but it was big, and it scared the crap out of me. I'm excited to see things because I've never been on a bayou, but at the same time, I'm glad I live in Washington. We don't have creepy crawlers in our waters."

"No kidding." I chuckle. God knows what she just saw. I've read there are all sorts of things in the waters here in the South, but I'm curious to see them all the same.

"Welcome." A man's booming voice catches our attention, and I feel Teagan startle once again. "I'm John. I'm your tour guide. Have ya filled out the necessary paperwork online? Or do ya need to come inside? We'll get ya set up in here. We're just waitin' on a few others to show before we get started."

"Hi, John. I'm Davis Fallon, and this is Teagan. I believe I filled everything out online." Glancing at Teagan, I find her nodding in agreement. "We should be set."

John looks over a list on a clipboard. "Sure enough. Got your names on the list. Shouldn't be long before the others arrive. Then we'll head out to the boat and get started with our tour. In the meantime, you're welcome to stay out here or go inside where the air is much cooler and enjoy our gift shop."

Teagan tilts her head toward the shop and says, "Thank you."

The moment we step inside what resembles an old shack

on the outside, I'm reminded of that saying about never judge a book by its cover. The building has been renovated and is obviously up to date with its air conditioning because I could be stepping into a surgical suite for as cool as the room feels. It's refreshing after the blistering Texas heat.

Teagan and I look around at the specialty souvenirs at the shop. There are key chains, trinkets, and a few t-shirts. With a stoic face, Teagan stops to hold up a neon-green t-shirt against her, *I'm the River Queen*. With her most regal expression, she touts, "What do ya think? Can I pull it off?"

She could pull off anything, but I pretend to think it over as I thumb through the shirts on the rack. This one might be better. "In light of what you saw earlier, this might be more appropriate..." I hold up a shirt that says *I only gamble when I'm floating the bayou.*

"Oh my God. That's perfect." She laughs as she snags it out of my hand to hold it against herself. "I might just have to get myself this one."

We browse for a few more minutes before making our way to the register near the door. When we pass by a table with blankets and baskets with an assortment of toys, Teagan stops once again. "Did your brother say what colors are in the nursery?"

I rack my brain to think if he's mentioned anything. "Nope. Can't say that he has. It's not the kind of thing we talk about," I admit in defense.

Lifting a few blankets, she pulls out a mint-green blanket with all sorts of textured tags sewn into the border. I know these are popular with infants and toddlers at the hospital. ""What do you think of this?" she asks with interest.

When she shakes the blanket to reveal its full size, I'm surprised to find it's bigger than most infant blankets. This one would be big enough for my niece for years to come. One side is a bumpy, soft fabric, and the other is the same fabric as the satin tags protruding out in every direction. "I think we may have a winner," I admit. "Both Melody and Tessa could fit under this for a while—at least until she outgrows it."

Not even looking at the price of the obviously handmade blanket, I take it from Teagan's hands. "This will be a hit for sure. I remember my nieces and nephews all having something like this—but much smaller. They were so sad when they outgrew them."

"I could snuggle in this blanket for days," Teagan admits with a grin. "Though not in this Texas heat. Maybe in the comforts of an air-conditioned room though."

"No kidding. I've lived here for two years, and I still forget how hot it can be when I venture outside the comforts of modern conveniences."

"What brought you to Texas?"

"Work." I shrug as I place the blanket on the counter to purchase.

A woman older than my mom kindly rings me up, and I throw in the t-shirt Teagan hasn't stopped carrying.

"Uh... I could get that," she protests after her shock wears off from me snagging it out of her hands.

"So can I." I grin mischievously before adding, "Besides—

how else are you going to remember your day with the stalker?"

Her mouth drops back as laughter fills the room. Shaking her head, she coughs out, "Oh, Davis—I don't think you're that forgettable."

I exaggerate as I purposely puff out my chest with confidence. "I guess I'll just have to make this day one you'll never forget."

A perfectly sculpted brow raises as she challenges, "I may just have to hold you to that."

The moment our purchases are in the bag, our tour guide returns. "Y'all ready?"

Before we walk to the tour boat, I quickly drop our purchases in the back of my Highlander and catch up with Teagan just as she gets to the boat. There are a few others ahead of her who must have arrived while we were shopping. Just as she's about to take a step from the dock to the tour boat, the boat shifts, and she hesitates.

On instinct, I reach out to steady her. "I've got you," I whisper so only she can hear.

Placing her hand on my extended arm, she holds it as she steps onto the boat, while I guide her at the small of her back with my other hand. Once she's settled, she lets go, and I feel a sudden loss.

She shoots me a smile as she whispers, "Thanks."

Thankfully, I don't have time to contemplate it because John announces what we'll expect on this tour.

"Once we're all seated, we'll get this show on the road!"

John booms. "Please keep your hands and feet inside the boat at all times—unless you'd like snapping turtles, alligators, or three-hundred-pound gars having you for a snack."

To this, Teagan visibly recoils from the reminder, and I find myself reaching out to squeeze her hand for reassurance. Wanting to give her the better view, I suggest she sit closest to the water.

Now, I'm regretting it. Maybe I should have taken the outside of the boat if she's not comfortable by the edge of the water.

Thankfully, John assures us we're safe—especially since we'll be moving. But Teagan still doesn't let go of my hand.

Not that I'm complaining.

Teagan's posture loosens a little once we move up the river, but from her grip, I can tell she's still on edge. John prattles on about the history of how his company came to be, but if I were to be quizzed on it later, I'd likely fail.

No, my focus has been on Teagan.

To get her to relax, I do something completely out of character for me. I gently switch hands and place an arm around her. At first, when she tenses up, I worry I've made the wrong decision. But as John talks, she settles against me, and she even laughs at something along the far shore of the river.

Now that I can smell her faint jasmine perfume with a hint of vanilla mixed in, she's all I can think about. Her skin is soft and though we've only met this morning, it somehow feels natural holding her. Small strands of hair escape her braid and blow around her face, and her face looks of wonder as John points things out and tells about the history of Deacon, Texas. I'm far more interested in what she's thinking about than life here on the bayou.

When we pass a large home on the side of the river, John points out that it once was the home of one of the first settlers but has been turned into a bed and breakfast by its current owner. The Monroe House Inn is what I think he called it. John's a natural storyteller and even though my thoughts never linger far from Teagan, I eventually find myself getting hooked on the history found along these riverbanks.

"Holy crap," Teagan whispers as she points to a log where a snapping turtle rests near the shore in the shade. "That's bigger than I thought." She scrambles into her purse to grab a picture before we pass by.

I'm not sure what I expected, but it's not something I'd want to encounter when swimming, as I grab my phone. "I'll stick to swimming pools," I mutter under my breath, not to interrupt John's latest story about the time he encountered a snapping turtle with his granddad as a kid.

"You and me both," Teagan agrees.

By the time we return from our tour, we've seen more turtles, alligators, and quite a few fish in the river. We even see some deer lying under a cypress tree. Being the tourists we are, phones are out and we take several pictures of the wildlife and some of the buildings we encounter. I'm not sure who has taken more on this trip—Teagan or me—but I'd be lying if I didn't sneak a few of her laughing in the process.

This woman is beautiful.

Thankfully, once Teagan relaxes, our playful banter

from this morning continues. Walking away from our tour guide, she hip-checks me and grins. "You know, if you want to be deemed as the favorite uncle, you may want to get a photo of you and that alligator in the background by the shore." She points to yet another alligator lazily lapping in the water.

"Uh, there's no way in hell I'm turning my back to that thing," I admit. "I consider myself adventurous but not stupid." It may be a good fifty feet away, but that's still too close to have my back turned for my liking.

Squeezing my hand, she admits, "Fair point. Besides, you got a few pictures they'll love from the boat."

As soon as we're back in my SUV, I realize I'm not ready for my time with her to end. Truth be told, I've been more relaxed today than I have in months, and I'm certain the beautiful bombshell sitting next to me has everything to do with it. "Wanna grab something to eat in town?"

"I could eat," she admits with a challenging grin that makes me want to kiss it right off her. "What do you have in mind?"

Quickly pondering our choices here in town, I let out a laugh. "I have no freaking clue. Should we drive down Main Street to see what's available?"

Reaching out to pat me on the leg as I drive, she smiles. "I think I could be up for that."

"Hopefully, we'll find something good."

Driving down Main Street, we find some of the diners are closed, but there are a few places open. Deacon isn't that big— so before we know it, we're on the other side of town, and I'm turning around. Of course, we still haven't decided. But riding with her, I don't mind retracing our steps.

"Welp, it looks like we have chicken or steak on the menu." Teagan chuckles. "The steak house might be too much food for this time of day; do you mind if we check out Kickin' Chicken?"

"I'm game for just about anything," I admit, then realize what I've said. "No pun intended."

As we pull into the parking lot, even though I see a drive-thru, I pull into a parking space. "Mind if we go in?" There's no way I'm ready to rush things along.

"Not at all—part of my me-cation involves slowing down and doing the things I never get to do."

What does that mean? "You don't eat out?"

If I weren't paying attention, I wouldn't have seen her brows knit and her lips purse. But as quickly as whatever she was thinking came on—it disappears with the shake of her head. On a long sigh, she says, "No. I don't get a lot of time to go out... well, I take that back. I drive through a lot of places—but never take the time to go inside and just enjoy a meal."

She is preaching to the choir. "You and me both," I start, then inspiration hits me. "Let's make a deal. Since we're both on a me-cation of sorts, let's spend the rest of the day doing all the things we never get the chance to do in our regular lives."

Her light-blue eyes dance with mischief as a smile plays on her lips. "You sure you wanna commit to that? You have no idea just how *little* life I have."

Chuckling lightly, I hedge, "It can't be that bad."

Teagan's chin lifts in challenge. "You may be in for a hell

of a lot more than you bargain for." Her eyes twinkle, and her confidence is sexy as hell, making me want to throw down a challenge of my own.

Just as I'm about to open the door to get out of my SUV, I look her in the eye. "I'm fairly certain I can handle just about anything you throw at me."

Chapter 4
Teagan

I'M FROZEN in place as Davis's words replay on a loop in my mind. *I'm fairly certain I can handle just about anything you throw at me.*

Holy hell. I'm certain he meant that in the most innocent way possible—but the way he looked at me had me heating in places I forgot existed.

Down, girl—he meant nothing by it.

There's no way in hell he'd know just how little I get to experience in my daily life.

But the thought of coloring outside the lines does sound intriguing.

Before I know it, he's at my door, and a warm burst of air flows through.

As Davis smiles down at me, all I can do is stare back in return, captivated by his handsome features as thoughts of all the things I haven't done in forever flood my mind. Before it gets awkward, I swear I hear Annie's voice whisper to me to *go for it!* The words jolt me out of my revelry.

Reaching for my hand, he helps me out of the car. That simple touch alone sends a bolt of electricity through my spine and has me eager to see what will come of the day. Instead of letting go of my hand, like I'd expect, he holds it until we get to the door.

A cold burst of air escapes as we walk inside. It's dark inside the entry compared to the brightness of the day, so it takes a moment for my eyes to adjust. When everything comes into focus, a life-size metal sculpture of a rooster stares back at me between the hostess stand and me, and I jump back in surprise.

"Well, cock-a-doodle-do to you," I mutter, trying not to bump into it.

"Well... that's just...." Davis's mouth drops open and closes as if he's unsure what to say.

"One giant cock?" I quickly supply. Then I throw my hands over my mouth. "Oh my God... I did not just say that."

But as I look around the restaurant, I see we're surrounded by more roosters than I can count. They're on the walls, decorating the walkways, as far as the eye can see. It's like I've stepped into Cracker Barrel but instead of antiques, the place is decorated with chickens. "Holy shit—they're everywhere!" The words escape before I think better of it.

"Well, you did say you wanted to get out of your comfort zone," Davis deadpans as he darts his eyes from display to display around the room.

Before we can contemplate further, a chipper woman comes up to greet us. "Howdy, welcome to Kickin' Chicken. Whether it's barbecued, grilled, stripped, or fried, we're bound to find a dish you're dying to try. Let me get you seated." She grabs two menus and some water glasses before walking in the direction of a table across the room.

Davis glances to me with wide eyes before placing a hand at the small of my back to guide me in her direction. Leaning in, he whispers, "Wonder how many times a day she has to say that?"

Stifling a laugh, I somehow manage to make it to our table without causing a scene.

Davis pulls out my chair and gets me settled, before taking a seat across from me. As we sit, we're told about today's specials: a Texas ranch casserole with collard greens and cornbread.

Once she leaves, Davis unexpectedly snorts, instantly grabbing my attention. "This is..." He looks further around the room, "something."

"What?" I ask, wanting to be clued in on his private joke.

"It's hard not to sound completely corny." Davis stiffens and does his best to school his features. "But why doesn't any man need more than one rooster?"

"Uhhh..." I draw out, trying to think of the answer. "I'll bite... Why?"

"A cock a dude'll do."

"Yeah. That's corny." I chortle. But the way his eyes crinkle at the corners and his lip twitches, I'd gladly hear a thousand more if he keeps looking at me that way.

Through a laugh, I challenge, "I tell one cock joke, and now I'll be bombarded with them—is that it?"

Davis just shrugs and looks back to the menu. "You could just tell me to cluck off, and I'll stop."

"You did not just say that," I say with a laugh. "Where are all the bad jokes coming from?"

"I'd like to say I'm that witty, but most are coming from this menu. Have you even looked at it, or is my charm too much for you to pay attention?"

I've been too focused on him to even look, but I'll never admit that. Since my menu is open, I finally focus on reading it. Sure enough, right above the salad selection, it says, *What do you call a rooster looking at lettuce? Chicken sees a salad.*

Oh my God. Seriously?

After reading a few others, I lock eyes with Davis, who's been watching me the entire time, and raise a brow in his direction. With as serious of a voice as I can muster, I ask, "So you're not usually this punny?"

Shaking his head, Davis sighs heavily. "I wish. I'm more of a smart ass and speak fluent sarcasm being the baby of my family. Though I've heard my share of dad jokes over the years. But come on, T, how can you *not* read some of these aloud?"

Sure enough, over the desserts, there is another doozy. But that doesn't stop me from voicing it aloud. "All right, Davis. You win. What do chickens serve at birthday parties?"

Exaggeratedly, he grins. "I don't know, Teagan. What *do they serve?*"

Grinning from ear to ear, like the dork I am, I smirk. "Coop-cakes."

"Have y'all decided?" The waitress eagerly interrupts with a pen and pad in hand. I'd been so focused on teasing Davis, I hadn't even seen her approach.

Davis clears his throat and glances at his menu. "I think I'll have the honey-glazed chicken sandwich with sweet potatoes and a side of asparagus."

My mouth waters at the thought of that. "Mmmm... that sounds amazing. I think I'll have the same. Can I also get an iced tea?"

"Sur'nuff. Sweet tea?" When I nod, she turns her attention to Davis, and he orders a Coke.

The moment she's gone, Davis's attention is back on me. I feel heat filter through my body just by his simple gaze alone. His jovial expression is still playful, yet there's more. I can't quite put my finger on it, but I'm excited to learn more.

Wanting to fill the silence, I quickly ask, "So... what's been your favorite part about Deacon so far?"

He smirks as his tongue runs quickly along his lower lip. That action alone makes me wonder what else he could do with that sexy mouth of his. Suddenly, he clears his throat, breaking me out of my fantasy, and he leans forward with his elbows on the table. "I'd have to say—meeting you."

"I bet you say that to all the women you stalk on your daily runs."

There's no way I'm the most interesting thing he's seen since arriving in this quaint little town.

Sighing heavily, he leans forward and takes my hand. Once he has my full attention, his voice is husky when he admits, "Seriously, Teagan, I haven't relaxed like this... since I don't know when. I'd be lying if I said I didn't think you were sexy as hell, but I've quickly found you're more than that. I love that you're unfiltered and share what's on your mind."

"Did you seriously go from poultry to sultry in two seconds flat? What makes me so special?"

For a second, he's silent. Then the table shakes, and a deep belly laugh rumbles from his body. "And apparently, you're not afraid to call me on my shit."

"You're damn straight I will," I retort, joining in the laughter.

"I'm gonna hold you to that," he quips.

Once I catch my breath, I lean forward on my elbows as well. "Seriously though, you barely know me. You don't even know what I do for a living."

"Nope—not going there. We both agreed to do things outside of our normal days. Work constitutes a daily task. We're both on me-cations. No work or anything work related today. I want to get to know you—the real you—not the you people perceive you as."

"Okay—so tell me this—what do you want to talk about if we aren't allowed to talk about work or daily routines?"

"For starters—you can tell me about the last time you did something for you and only you?"

I think about this for a long moment, then I throw my hands in the air and admit, "Holy shit. I have no idea."

"Tell me this—when was the last time you went on a date?"

I look to the sky, hoping for some divine intervention— that's even been longer. "Uh... let's just say it's been awhile. Hell, I wouldn't even know what to do on a date."

Davis raises a brow. "Uh... you seem to be doing just fine today."

Wait... This is a date?

Holy shit.

He's right.

I'm so freaking out of the game, I haven't even recognized I'm on a date.

I need to get out more.

He must read the deer-in-headlights expression on my face when he suddenly cringes. "Did I... uh... read this wrong? I've enjoyed getting to know you and have been thinking of ways to keep my time with you from ending."

"No... I'm enjoying our time together. I'm just rusty... and apparently, I have zero game."

"So, you agree—this is a date?" he hedges in challenge.

I guess my dirty thoughts have been appropriate. He does think of me as a date. Maybe I haven't lost it after all?

Davis's grin is wide when he drawls out, "Oh, Teagan, you should wait until we're alone before voicing those thoughts... I can't wait to hear what they are."

"Holy shit, I said that aloud."

Chapter 5
Davis

TEAGAN'S FACE turns brighter than an overripe tomato. Now that I know she's having dirty thoughts about me, I don't feel nearly as bad for thinking them in return. Hell, she's held my attention since I spotted her on our run this morning, and I have no intention of letting our time together end anytime soon.

Thankfully, she can't respond because our waitress returns with our meal, and we're both suddenly busy eating the delicious food. Everything today has been so fun and easy with Teagan, but I wonder if I took things too far with that comment. When she breaks the silence, I know things are good between us.

"You know, you're in luck. If we're only doing things out of our ordinary day today, a date is definitely on that list. I can't wait to see what we do next."

"We'll manage something," I assure her, as I fork an asparagus spear before taking another bite. "There's gotta be something in this town we haven't done in a while."

Tipping her head to the side, she asks, "You mean like

eating a meal in a room filled with thousands of cocks is ordinary for you?"

I nearly spit my drink in her face as her long lashes blink at me in feign innocence. "I can say with certainty, this is the most I've ever been around." Teagan may feel rusty, but this woman is a vixen, and I like it.

As we leave the restaurant, Teagan insists we stop to take a photo with a giant cock between us. The thing is taller than she is and rivals me. Our laughter never stops as our waitress takes photos with our phones. Once she returns our phones, I pull Teagan to my side. As she stares into my eyes, I want nothing more than to kiss her. But before I can make a move, another couple walks in and our moment is lost.

Eager to continue our date, I reach for her hand and guide her to the door.

When we get to the car, instead of opening the door, I pull up short, making her turn to face me. With her body just inches from mine, it would be so easy to simply lower my head and press my lips to hers. As we stare at one another, the tension between us takes on a physical presence. I'm dying to know what her lips feel like.

Just as I step a little closer, her mouth tilts up and splits into a wide grin. "What's next on the agenda? I'm sure with this being a weekday, the sidewalks roll up in this town, but if we're lucky, we'll find something to do tonight."

I swear I wasn't imagining our connection but suddenly, our conversation from earlier comes to mind. "Hey, Teagan?"

Doe eyed, she asks, "What?"

"You're doing it again."

Complete confusion crosses her features. "Doing what?"

"Being oblivious."

She's silent for a moment and appears to be concentrating on what I've said. Then suddenly, she gasps and darts her eyes to my lips, as if she finally gets what I'm saying.

The second she darts her tongue out to wet her bottom lip, I know I can't wait any longer. Leaning in, I press my lips to hers.

At first, Teagan freezes, and I worry I've made a mistake.

But before I can pull away, her hands grasp the base of my neck and pull me closer, so our bodies are flush against one another. The moment she opens her mouth to me, I let my tongue slip inside and truly taste her.

It's like a live wire surges up my spine, and heat explodes throughout my entire body. I simply can't get enough. My hand slides along her spine until one hand settles at the base of her neck, allowing me to guide and deepen our kiss. Teagan responds with a sense of urgency, making me forget everything but her.

The car next to us chirps to disarm its alarm, causing us to jump apart in surprise. Breathless and panting for air, I dart my eyes around the parking lot, in search of its owner.

Thankfully, it's an elderly couple just exiting the building, so our public display of affection isn't blocking them from their car. When my eyes return to Teagan, I find her cheeks pink and a giggle escaping her lips. "I... uh, think we'd better get going," she says, watching the couple approach.

Wordlessly, I open her door, and she hops in. Since it's still warm, I quickly rush to the other side and slide in beside her to start the car. Both of us keep our eyes on the road as I silently drive out of the parking lot.

Once we're out of sight from the restaurant, Teagan breaks the silence with a chuckle. "Did we really get so lost in the moment, a car alarm had to remind us we're in public?"

"Yep. I believe it did." And I most certainly hope it happens again.

"Oh, look, they're doing karaoke tonight. I haven't done that since college."

"Looks like we've found our plans for the evening. Mind if we stop by the B&B? I'd like to change into a pair of jeans."

"Not at all. I'll probably change my shoes and make a quick call."

Hand in hand, we walk inside Tilly's. Since it's on my way, I walk her to her door. But before she opens it, she turns to face me. Her expression is soft as she pins me with her beautiful eyes. "In case I forget to tell you, I'm having a great time today."

Reaching to push a lock of wayward hair behind her ear, I have a visceral need to pull her in and kiss her once more. "Same," I murmur, closing the small distance between us.

The moment my lips touch hers, a low groan escapes her mouth as she tugs on my lower lip with her teeth. Fuck, if that doesn't go straight to my straining dick. Teagan is the perfect combination of sexy and sweet and with any luck, I'll spend the rest of my vacation with her.

If I don't walk away now, we'll never leave this hallway. I reluctantly slow our kiss and force myself to slow things down. Through a smile as I kiss her lips once more, I whisper, "Go make your phone call." Kiss. "Just come to my room when you're ready." Another kiss.

"Okay." Her words come out breathless. Then she pulls me in for one last kiss. "I'll see you in a bit."

Finally, I move away from her. I turn and don't look back, or I'll likely walk into her room and make other plans for our evening.

Inside my room, I realize the Coke and bottled water I'd brought with me in my bag of snacks never made it to the fridge. I groan in frustration. There's no way I want to drink warm soda while I wait for her. Remembering the ice machine in the breakfast area, I grab the bucket on the cabinet and quickly rush to fill it.

I'm back within a few minutes, and Teagan is nowhere in sight. Grabbing a plastic cup from the cabinet, I fill it with ice. In my haste, I knock my can of Coke over. Instinctually, I flick the side of the can to see if I can keep from having it erupt all over me.

As I slowly crack the seal, I quickly realize it wasn't enough. "Oh, shit." I gasp as soda explodes everywhere, spraying me directly in the face and soaking my shirt. I try my best to cover it with my hand, but I'm just making a bigger mess.

When it finally stops gushing like Old Faithful, I'm a sticky, hot mess—and not in a good way. "Fuck me to hell. I need a shower."

Grabbing some towels from the bathroom, I quickly wet one and do my best to wipe up the mess on the cabinet and hardwood, then dry it with another. Thank God this place wasn't carpeted.

Shit, I'm burning precious time. Rushing to the bathroom, I throw the towels on the floor and jump into the shower. Within a few minutes, I'm clean and standing before my suitcase, wrapped in only a towel as I dig through my clothes. I quickly slip on my boxer briefs and a pair of jeans. Just as I get them zipped, there's a knock at my door.

Not wanting to make Teagan wait, I rush to open it.

In a split second, her face morphs from a smile to an "o" as her jaw drops, and her eyes travel across my body.

"Come on in," I rush out. "Sorry I'm not ready, but my Coke exploded, and I had to shower. It'll only take a second to be ready."

Her mouth shuts, then opens again as her eyes focus on my abdomen. I look down, and I'm embarrassed to realize I don't even have my fly buttoned. When I return my gaze to her, I'm surprised to see she's frozen in place. "Teagan? Would you rather wait out here?"

"What?" she asks shakily.

"Wanna come in or wait out here while I get ready?" I ask, stepping further into my room.

Slowly closing her eyes, she mutters, "I... Uh... I'll come in."

"You sure?" I ask with hesitation because she's still frozen in place, and I don't want to force anything on her.

She's adorable as she shakes her head and sucks in a breath loudly. Clearly, I'm affecting her—and I'm not sure it's in a bad way. Her eyes fill with heat, and it takes everything in my power not to step in and kiss that expression off her face.

Eventually, words sputter from her. "No… I'll… come in."

Chuckling, I tease, "I'd better put on a shirt." Turning, I rush to my suitcase and grab the first one I can find.

"Or don't," she says quickly from behind me.

When I turn back to her, she's standing much closer than I expect.

Teeth sunken into her lower lip, her long lashes dip to the floor before she looks me in the eyes. With a boldness I'm growing to love, she steps closer. "We agreed this was a day we do things out of the ordinary and right now… in this moment, all I want is to kiss every square inch of your body."

Holy. Fucking. Hell.

Her determination is sexy as sin when she reaches for me. The moment her hand touches my face to pull me closer, my cock twitches, and my senses zing into overdrive. My lips crash onto hers, and I pull her body close to mine.

Our kisses had been consuming before. But now, we've become an inferno. Each kiss, caress, and touch are like drops of gasoline on a fire. A roar escapes as I devour her mouth. She tastes of mint and sin in the best possible way.

I. Am. In. Heaven.

When her fingers roam along my blazing skin, every nerve ending comes to life. Needing to feel her, my fingers roam along her spine, under her ass, and along the skirt of her dress, to her exposed thigh that's wrapped around my jean-clad leg. Her skin is silky smooth as I hike her dress up her leg.

With her hand resting on my chest for balance, she breaks

our kiss, trailing her lips along my jaw to my collarbone, setting my need for her on fire. Time stands still as I savor these sensations and just be in this moment with her. Her trail of wet, hot kisses burn my skin in their wake, and I want more.

Trailing my fingers up to her thigh, I grip her ass, pulling her closer. When her head tips up, and she looks me in the eye, my lips crash onto hers once again. Sliding her hands to the back of my neck, her fingers tickle my scalp as she runs them through the short hairs. And fuck if that doesn't send my body into hyperdrive. If the sounds she elicits when I deepen our kiss are any indication of her thoughts, it's clear we're entirely on the same page.

Gripping her ass, I lift her effortlessly. A small gasp escapes her, and she breaks our kiss to look me in the eye. But the moment I walk us to the nearest wall, she clutches her arms around my shoulders and her legs around my hips to cling to me as if she's trying to help with the nonexistent burden of her weight. Her efforts are unnecessary, but before I can utter a syllable, her lips return to mine, and all thoughts of conversation disappear.

The moment her back hits the wall, the skirt of her dress pools at her lap, leaving full access for my fingers to glide up her silky-smooth legs. Trailing kisses down the column of her neck, I feel before I hear her moan escape, which only turns me on further. Tracing her panties from her ass to her hip, she grinds against me and practically begs, "Please…"

She tastes magnificent as I kiss down the swell of her breast. I vow, "Tell me what you want, and it's yours."

"You," she moans.

Leaning back to look her in the eye, I challenge, "You gotta be more specific."

Wide eyed, she just stares. If we're sticking to challenging ourselves to do things out of the normal, she needs to vocalize this.

When I simply stare, determined to out-wait her, she mutters, "I... uh... just want you."

I still hold her gaze silently, though I raise a brow in challenge.

"I liked what you were doing and want to know where you plan to go next."

Oh, I like that, too. The thought alone has me imagining all the things I can do to her with only my fingers.

Before I can reply, she quickly huffs out, "How do you expect me to think when you've gotten me all hot and bothered?"

Leaning in, I kiss her fervently in reward. Just as I'm about to end our kiss, I playfully tug at her lower lip with my teeth, before I promise, "Oh, I'm just getting started, Teagan."

Her beautiful laugh fills the room. "Well, then—show me what you've got."

Oh, I'll show her all right.

Chapter 6

Teagan

AS IF I'VE thrown down the gauntlet, Davis's eyes fill with liquid heat, as his expression darkens. A shiver runs through my body in anticipation of what's to come. Just that look alone has my core flooding with heat and my heart racing.

Sliding a hand up my ribs to cup my breast, he squeezes, making my nipples so hard, they could cut glass. When his lips return to the swell of my breast, his hot kisses along my skin make my breath quicken.

God. It's been forever since I've felt the touch of a man.

It feels incredible as he swirls his tongue around my hard tip, then sucks more of me into his mouth. The moment his teeth scrape along my sensitive flesh, everything deep inside me clenches and electricity zips through every nerve ending.

When a finger traces the center of my folds and presses against my clit, I can't even be ashamed of how wet I am. Davis should be damn proud of how he's gotten my body zinging into overdrive in a nanosecond. I don't think anyone's ever gotten me so close to tipping over the edge of ecstasy in such a short time.

It feels heavenly grinding against his palm as he presses

against my mound, all while his long fingers tease me. Still on the outside of the fabric, they slide along my folds to my center and back up. He's got me so close—but it's not quite enough. "More..." I pant, remembering he asked me to be vocal. "I need more, Davis."

Releasing the suction on my breast, his lips never leave my flesh as he demands with a growl, "More of what? Tell me what you need."

When he sucks my nipple back into his mouth and tweaks the tip with his skillful tongue and nips his teeth into my skin, I can't even remember my name. "Fuck, that feels amazing." Especially when he applies pressure to my clit.

Through nips and swirls and tugs, he murmurs, "I want words, T. Tell me what you need."

"I want..." I pant and then moan as he flicks my nipple with his tongue. "I need you... inside me."

A rumble flows through his chest as he practically growls, "All you had to do is ask, T."

Simultaneously, he flicks my nipple as his fingers find their way under the fabric, and one long finger slips inside me.

"Holy. Shit... Yes. Right there," I pant when the pad of his thumb rolls along my clit, and his fingers slide in and out of my slickness. It's all I can do to not scream out in pleasure.

I feel my orgasm just on the edge of reach. My spine tightens, and my senses go on overdrive. His teeth biting as he tugs on my breast is the most delicious sensation. When he adds more fingers into the mix, I'm flying over the edge faster than I could imagine.

Wave after wave of explosive heat flows through me, and I

never want this moment to end. Needing this to last, I focus on my fullness and the muscles clenching around his fingers and ride out this high to its fullest extent. When I can't last another second, I let go to the sensations building. My vision blurs as I throw my head back and dig my hands into his hair to guide his continued nipple play.

Holy shit, this man knows what he's doing.

As tremor after tremor rock my body, he releases my heavy breast and kisses his way back up my neck. Once his tongue meets mine, I somehow find the energy to kiss him back for all I'm worth. His tongue is wicked as his skilled fingers continue to strum me in perfect rhythm, plucking out every last twitch of my orgasm.

Eventually, he rests his forehead on mine, and his fingers slip from my folds. Our breaths are ragged as we stare at one another.

In this moment, looking into Davis's eyes, I've never felt so intimate and at peace with another human.

No words are needed as he watches me come down from my high, and we find ourselves breathing in unison. Each rise and fall of our chests bring us one breath closer to returning to a normal tempo. Eventually, he lets my legs fall, but not before he knows I can stand on my own.

Keeping me pinned to the wall, he kisses me once more before he asks, "Would you still like to go out tonight? Or could I interest you in something else?"

Acting much bolder than I feel, I boldly ask, "And just what do you have in mind?"

Tipping his head back in laughter, he smirks. "I don't have a set plan, but I know it'll involve many more orgasms—starting with you coming next on my mouth."

Bringing my finger to my chin, I pretend there's even a choice. "Hmmm... More orgasms—starting with your mouth. I think I can get on board with that."

With a wicked grin, he practically growls, "Good, because I'm dying to know how you taste."

Holy shit. Did he just say that?

"I've never... I mean, I have... but I've never had someone seem so excited for *that* before." The words fly out of my mouth before I can rein in my thoughts. Shit. Can't I keep some things to myself?

"Then you don't know what you're missing," he says. Tugging me close for another sensual kiss—though not as fervent as before, yet it's still filled with passion, makes my toes curl. Eventually, we break apart, and he reaches for my hand as he squeezes it.

"What do you mean—you've never?" he asks, leading me to the edge of the bed and sitting. "If we're keeping things out of the ordinary—I need to know what you're used to—and more important—what you like. I want to make this as good for you as I can."

I don't even know how to begin to answer that question. It's been so long since I've been with a man, do I even know what I like?

Reaching out a thumb, he releases my lower lip from my teeth. "What's wrong, Teagan? Talk to me."

Releasing the breath I didn't know I'd been holding, I shyly admit, "It's been a long time."

Squeezing my hand, he smiles reassuringly. "From my understanding, it's like getting on a bike, right?"

The way he says it isn't condescending in the slightest. The sincerity in his expression shows he holds no judgement. But he wants me to be honest with him. After all, if we're not honest, how will we know what the other likes? That alone is something out of the ordinary for me—so I might as well embrace this opportunity.

Then reality strikes, and I find myself admitting, "Well, I haven't been with anyone who has enjoyed focusing on my pleasure—in since... well, forever," I quickly admit. "Especially someone who gets me out of my head—so I can actually have more than one orgasm."

His jaw drops unexpectedly. "What do you mean?"

How the hell do I say this without sounding as if I'm defective? "I've... sorta been known for being one and done—so don't feel disappointed if I don't get there again anytime soon."

"Okay, so you get stuck in your head. We can work with that."

How does he know that?

Leaning in, he kisses the shocked expression from my face.

When we break apart, he squeezes my hand and shrugs as if he's a mind reader. "With as responsive as you are, I have my doubts about you being one and done tonight. But even if that *is* the case, I have some great ideas that will be exciting as hell to try."

This does the trick. All the reservations I'd suddenly created in my head disappear.

"First, we have to stick to the rule of you telling me what you like. If there's something you don't like—or you find yourself disengaging, you have to let me know immediately, so I can change my tactics."

Even though I've known him less than a day, his boldness and open communication make me feel in this moment that I can trust him implicitly. "Okay."

"Next, I know we've just met, but I have an idea for you to only feel what I'm about to do for you…"

"Okay…" I draw out, hoping he'll explain more.

"Do you think you'd be able to trust me enough to find a way to stay focused on what you're feeling, rather than what you're thinking?"

"That sounds…" Hell, I'm not even sure what that means.

Do I trust him?

All it takes is one look into his eyes, and I know without a doubt. I do.

Why is it harder to admit that to him?

So, I quickly add, "Doable," before I can a) chicken out or b) sound like a complete idiot.

"Okay." He grins so sexily that my core clenches at just the thought of those sexy lips on me. "As much as I think this is a beautiful dress…" He reaches for the hem of the skirt. "It's gotta go."

Emboldened by the way he makes me feel, I reach for the hem and help him take it over my head. When I realize I'm in nothing but my bra and undies, I look to his jeans. "But those gotta go, too."

He lets out a low breath. "Oh, trust me, they'll be gone. But I want to taste you properly first. You threw down a challenge, and I'm dying to see if I can rise to your expectations."

"Okay, then, what do you have in mind?"

Leaning in, he kisses me once more. But instead of laying me back on the bed like I expect, he jumps up and rushes to his suitcase.

"Where the heck are you going?" I ask to his back.

"You'll see," he says as he unzips something and turns to face me.

"Are you thirsty?" he asks, reaching for a glass and fills it with ice before adding a fresh can of Coke.

Seriously? That's what he thinks I want right now?

"Uh, not really."

Taking a large gulp of Coke, he refills the glass as if he doesn't have a care in the world, then asks, "You sure?" He reaches for something in his suitcase, but before I can see what it is, he turns and walks toward me with one hand behind his back and stuffs it into his pocket.

Walks is an inept description.

This sexy man stalks to me as if he's on the hunt, and I'm his eager prey. There's nothing scary about him; rather his gait is strong and expression sensual as he reaches for my face. Leaning in, his cool lips reach mine, and I can feel the effects of the ice in his mouth as he greedily kisses me. "Hmmmm, you taste amazing." Pulling back, he reaches for my hand to help me stand. "Let's scooch you back on the bed and get you comfortable. I plan on taking my time with you, and I want to make use of this king-sized bed."

Turning, I find myself crawling up the bed in excitement. Once I reach the pillows, I return to face him, getting comfortable as he requested. My body's filled with need, and my core clenches as I look to see him watching me with desire written all over his face. "You see something you like?" I tease.

"Oh, Teagan." His voice is low and filled with want. "There isn't one thing I haven't liked about you so far."

The bed dips as his knee presses into the mattress, and I feel him crawl up my body. When he gets to my thigh, he stops to lick his tongue up my inner leg to my underwear. But instead of going directly for the mark he's promised, he skips over my clothing and kisses up my stomach to my ribs.

I'm ticklish, but the sensations he brings are more than that. Pulses of electrical currents flow from my core, up my spine, and down my legs. Reaching between my breast, he unclasps my bra and lets it fall open, exposing me to him.

Needing to touch him, I run my fingers along the base of his neck and let that prickly sensation wash over me. I've missed running my hands through a man's hair as he devours my body. Davis's hair is short and tight on the sides and tapers to being long at the top. Just the perfect amount to grab on to, in my opinion.

With his mouth playing with my pert nipples, his fingertips run along my inner thigh, touching me everywhere, but where I want it most. "Davis," I groan in protest when he skips over my core and sweeps down my thigh again.

Pulling back, he stares at me for a long moment, while his hands continue their lazy perusal. His stare is so intent, I'm not sure what to make of it. Has he changed his mind? I'd never want him to do something he doesn't want. "If you've—" I start, but he puts a finger over my lips to stop me from saying more.

"Get out of your head." He waits until I relax once again before adding, "I have an idea..."

He looks... is that unsure? No, it can't be. When I can't take it any longer, I ask, "What is it?"

Grinning, he leans in for a quick kiss before he hovers over me once more. "I have a way that would ensure you're only focusing on the sensations you feel, rather than getting stuck in your head." He reaches into his back pocket and pulls out a navy necktie.

"You want to tie me up?" I ask in disbelief, yet aroused at the thought.

Chuckling, he shakes his head. "Someday—sure. If you're into that. But today, I'd like to use it as a blindfold. I've read that when one sensory input is cut off, others intensify. I thought we could use this to make sure I keep you out of your head."

I just stare as I take in his words.

"If you're not into this, that's fine. I thought I'd try something new for me, too."

This is new for him?

The fact that he's going to such great lengths to make sure my needs are met is both enduring and more than a turn-on. Nodding, I agree, and my body sizzles in anticipation of being blindfolded. I've read books about this—but have never experienced it. Wanting to try new things with Davis, I lean forward and urge, "Let's do this."

As soon as the tie is secure, and all I can see is blackness, there's a buzz in the air as I wonder what he'll do first. I feel the bed dip as he repositions himself to kiss me tenderly on the lips. "For this to work, you'll need to talk to me, Teagan."

Nodding, I agree.

"Words, Teagan. I'm gonna need them. Soon, I won't be able to read your face, and I want to make this the best I can for you."

"Okay."

Feeling his fingers dip into the edge of my underwear at my hips, he asks, "Can I take these off?"

"Yes," I whisper with another nod.

As he reveals my pussy, I feel his cool breath blow across my sensitive skin. "Ohhh...." I moan. "That feels incredible."

A finger dips into me for the briefest of seconds, then traces up my folds to my clit, just as his tongue flicks my nipple expertly.

Holy shit. I like that.

He sets a slow rhythm, dragging his finger in and out of me, tracing my folds, then circling my clit. As if he doesn't have a care in the world, he continues this pattern until I'm squirming like crazy beneath him.

Eventually, the bed moves as he repositions himself further down my body.

Trailing kisses down my rib cage to my hips, he kisses across my body, leaving a fire in his wake. When he reaches my hip, he scrapes his teeth on my skin, and I buck in approval. His breath hovers over my mound, but before he does anything, I feel his tongue run along my inner thigh.

The bed dips again, and I think he's finally going to put an end to my torture.

But suddenly, he's gone.

I start to sit up, but in a stern voice, he says, "Don't move."

"But..." I protest, but I'm cut off.

"How do you like the blindfold?" I hear from across the room.

I think about how to respond. "I like it," I finally admit on a sigh. "I love not knowing what you're going to do next."

"Good. That's exactly the point." I can hear the smile in his voice. "Mind if I add another element of surprise?"

Racking my brain, I try to think of what he might be suggesting.

"It's either yes or no." His firm voice demands. "Stay out of your head. I just saw you tense. I'm fine either way—just want to know if I can add something you might enjoy."

"What if I don't like it?" I ask hesitantly, needing to make sure we're on the same page; even I can't imagine this man doing anything I wouldn't enjoy.

As if he isn't bothered at all by the question he simply says, "Then we stop. Simple as that. My only focus is to get you out of your head, not make you uncomfortable in any way. That's why communication is key."

Get out of your head, T. If he thinks I'll enjoy it, why object? Nodding profusely, I say, "Okay, surprise me."

His deep chuckle has my core clenching and nipples tightening.

I hear ice pour into a glass, and Davis takes another slow sip of Coke.

"You're so fucking beautiful," he says much closer than I expect as he sets a glass on the bedside table by my head.

The next thing I know, something cold shocks the hell out of me as it circles my nipple.

Holy shit, he's using ice.

"Shhh..." he encourages. "If you don't like it, I'll stop."

The moment his lips trace the trail of the ice, I know this is the hottest thing I've ever experienced. I quickly blurt out, "Don't stop... I just wasn't expecting that."

Chuckling, I can hear his smile as he reminds me, "That's kinda the point."

He's quiet for a moment as he resettles between my legs. Reaching for the cup, I hear him replace it on the table before I feel him once more. This time, instead of my breast, he's trailing it down my stomach and across my belly button. Once again, his warm tongue traces the blazing trail of the ice cube. "Talk to me, T. What do you like?"

"I love the mix of hot and cold against my skin. I love that I never know what you're going to do next, and I don't want you to stop," I point out, realizing my talking is making the sensation wain.

"Okay, point taken." The cup moves again, and he says, "I'm going to be *very occupied* for the next bit. But I need you to stay vocal. Nothing turns me on more than a woman expressing her needs."

Okay, so he likes it vocal. I guess I can try to comply.

Dipping a finger straight into my center, I jump from the sudden coolness. But before I can do anything, his finger retreats, and his warm breath replaces the sensation.

"Oh. My. Fucking God," I curse, clenching the sheets to keep me in place when he dips his tongue inside me and runs it along my seam to my clit. Using his warm fingers, he spreads my folds to gain access. Just as he did with my nipples, he circles my clit and sucks it into his mouth.

I'm not even sure what I mutter in appreciation because the moment he sticks another warm finger inside me, I no longer have coherent words. Sliding it in and out, my body adjusts as it warms with our friction. The moment his finger disappears, an icy tongue circles my clit.

Instead of freezing me, like I'd expect, it somehow burns me from the inside out. Every nerve ending comes alive and heats me from my core as his kisses return to hot with time. When his lips leave my clit, instead of a cool finger slipping into my center, an entire ice cube slides in with his fingers, making me gasp in surprise.

Holy shit. There's an ice cube in me.

It distinctly moves and shifts along my inner walls as he quickens the pace with multiple fingers to warm me up. The mixture of hot and cold has me bucking up from the bed, and I can't get enough of this sensation.

Pressing a forearm over my abdomen to keep me in place, I hear his smile as he asks, "You like that?"

I don't even have to think when I practically shout, "Do that again."

I need to feel it again. It feels so sexy with a side of kink I never knew existed. Apparently, I've only had boring and functional sexual experiences to this point. Who knew there was a whole other world I've been deprived of?

Taking my clit in his mouth, he sucks hard as another ice cube slips in with masterful fingers. This time, he swoops it against my inner wall, then presses his finger along it to warm up as it slips off into another location behind his hand.

As his tongue traces along my seam and back to my clit, my body unexpectedly tenses. Then his finger hits a place inside me I've never known existed and simultaneously, his lips curl around my clit. All it takes is one suck, and I'm flying into oblivion.

I swear, if I wasn't blindfolded, I'd still be unable to see as my eyes roll to the back of my head as pulse after pulse of an earth-shattering orgasm spreads to every part of my body. Hell, my fingers and toes lose sensation. Of course, Davis doesn't leave me hanging. He milks every tremor of my orgasm out of me.

When I'm nothing but a puddle of goo, I feel the blindfold be removed, and the room fills with light. When I finally do regain focus, I feel Davis's body pressed against me and find his beautiful eyes staring into mine.

With a wicked grin, he leans in to kiss me once before pulling back to look me in the eyes. "Welcome back. As much as I fucking loved doing that to you, I've missed seeing these beautiful, expressive eyes."

"I think you've broken me," I whisper because that's all the energy I have left.

"In the best possible way, I hope."

"Definitely." I nod. "I guess I'm not actually broken after all, as you've just given me two outstanding Os back-to-back."

"Would you like to see how I plan to get a third one out of you?"

Somehow, my well-spent libido springs back to life. "Oh, do tell."

"Well…" He leans in to give me a slow, lingering kiss. We taste of sex and us and just thinking of that makes my inner muscles clench and electricity zip through me. "I think it will start with me slowly sliding inside you. Then when you're ready, I'm dying for you to ride me. I can't wait to have these heavenly tits hanging in my face as you have your wicked way with me."

Holy shit, how can I be ready for round three already?

SOMEHOW, I lose track of just how many orgasms he works out of me. The next thing I know, I'm woken to the sound of a phone ringing. Reaching for the bedside, I realize it's not where I usually leave it. Crawling out of bed, I realize I'm alone but see a big note by my purse as I reach for my phone.

Smiling, I read his note:

**We've missed breakfast, gone to the bakery
to grab us something.
Be back as soon as I can,
D**

How sweet is this man?

This is the last moments of bliss I experience before the glorious bubble we've existed in, bursts.

Connecting the call, a frantic voice comes through. "Teagan? Are you there?"

Instantly, I'm on alert as I reply, "Yeah, I'm here."

"It's Connor. He needs you."

Chapter 7
Davis

WALKING into the Bean Brew Café, I admire the exposed bricks and concrete ceilings. My brother Damien, the civil engineer, would appreciate how the owner's renovated this old firehouse. There are still fire poles, but instead of fire engines at the ready, there are tables and chairs scattered for patrons to enjoy.

When I step to the counter, an older gentleman greets me, "Mornin', what can I get for you?"

"I'll take the largest cup of your darkest coffee and a medium cinnamon mocha." Spotting some danishes in the display case in front of me, I say, "I'll also take two danishes and two egg and cheese sandwiches."

"Coming right up. I'm Rex. I don't think I've seen you in before," he says as he rings up my order.

Reaching out to shake his hand, I introduce myself. "Davis. I'm only in town for a short trip. Are you the owner?"

"Yeah." He nods as a girl behind him makes my order. "When I retired as fire chief, the city built a new fire station. I just couldn't not come to this place every day."

"You've done a great job on the renovations," I admit. "I love what you've done to the place."

"Thanks. Some would call it a passion project, but I spent years keeping this place in top shape. Just because I'm no longer fighting fires doesn't mean I've given up on this beauty of a building."

When another customer enters, I quickly step to the side and let him wait on her.

Once my order is ready, Rex calls over to me, "Davis, your order is ready. Enjoy the rest of your visit to Deacon."

The man has a great memory. Grabbing my food, I make my way to my SUV.

Carrying our food from the car into the building is simple enough. When I realize I've left my key to the room in my wallet, I'll admit I'm less than graceful retrieving it. Finally, after almost spilling the coffee and mocha, I give up and set the drink carrier on the floor as well as our bag of food. I dig out the key from my wallet.

Opening the door as quietly as I can, I smile at the memory of last night. She'd just gone down on me and had the devilish grin once she realized how quick she could make me come with that wicked tongue of hers. She'd looked over at the window as she fell back onto the bed. "I'm going to need the largest cinnamon mocha they have in this town. I haven't been up until the sun rose since college."

I'd quickly kissed her as I pulled her into my side and assured her, "Relax. Neither of us have anywhere we need to be today. I'll make sure you have your needed dose of caffeine."

It's nearly noon, and the room is still dark as the blackout curtains are still drawn. It takes a moment for my eyes to adjust to my surroundings.

She must be out since she doesn't stir when I turn on the bathroom light. Since I've already drunk most of my coffee, I take it into the bathroom and decide to take a quick spin in the shower, while I wait for her to wake up.

After a steamy hot shower, I feel refreshed and ready for the day. After drying off, I wrap a towel around me and walk to my suitcase.

It's then I realize the bed is empty, and Teagan is nowhere to be found.

Maybe she decided to shower back at her place? She must have seen the note I left on the top of her purse, and since both are missing, I'll just give her some time to return.

Wanting to make the most of our time together, I quickly dress and grab our food, intent on eating it and her again for breakfast.

I walk the necessary steps to her room and knock.

Nothing.

Knocking again, I press my ear to the door.

Still nothing.

What the fuck is going on?

I'd call her, but I didn't even think to get her fucking number yesterday. Nope. I was too busy, *enjoying the moment* to be bothered with thinking about needing it.

I walk to the dining area to see if she's there but no such luck.

Thinking maybe she's in the shower, I knock once again when I get to her door.

"Teagan? Are you there?" I holler through the door.

But still nothing.

Then another thought hits me.

Holy shit, what if last night didn't mean the same to her? I swear she was into me, but maybe this was just a one-night stand to her, and I'm being blown off.

Thinking about the way we talked and snuggled between rounds of pleasure, my gut knows that isn't the case—but where the hell is she?

Sulking, I return to my room.

The place still smells of her perfume, and the disarray of the blankets on the bed makes my memories from last night repeat on a loop. Every kiss, every laugh, and every confession felt so real. I swear our connection was real.

But after two more days, what would come of it?

She's going back to Washington, and I'm stuck here, dumbass.

Maybe she realized things have gotten too real and decided to bolt before I could dismiss her—like everyone I've been with since realizing becoming a doctor was my dream. It's probably for the best that she leaves. It's not like I'm good at long-term relationships.

Before I can contemplate this much further, my phone rings with the on-call tone I've given the hospital to take note of emergencies.

"This is Davis Fallon."

A sweet, Southern voice comes through the phone. "I'm

sorry to bother you on your vacation, but Dr. Jamison's wife has gone into labor, and we need a consult for a four-year-old male who appears to have fractured their olecranon. It's close to the growth plate, and the physician on call would like a consult before casting to determine if surgery is necessary."

Immediately, my hand goes to my elbow as I rub the protruding bone she speaks of.

"I'm about thirty-five to forty minutes away from the hospital. I can be there within the hour. Please reach out to Hannah Brighton, my intern, and fill her in on this. Tell her when to expect me. I'll be looking forward to having her get me up to date with the further needs of the patient when I arrive. I'd like to keep the family waiting as little as possible. Please let them also know I'm on my way."

"Will do, sir."

"Thank you."

And with that, my vacation is officially over.

I quickly rush to the bathroom and gather my things to stuff them into my suitcase. Thank goodness I hadn't unpacked because this case will keep me busy for the next day or so, and I'm scheduled to work the remainder of the week.

Walking past Teagan's door, I knock once more, but it's a futile attempt as it remains unanswered. Stopping at the front desk, I ring the bell and wait for assistance. It doesn't take long before the woman who served us breakfast yesterday appears.

"How can I help you?"

"I have an emergency I need to get to Austin for. Is it possible to leave a note for another guest with you?"

When she nods in approval, I quickly grab a piece of paper from a pad on the counter and scribble out a note.

Teagan,
I had a work emergency and had to return
to Austin unexpectedly.
Please call me when you get this.
D

I read it twice before adding my number to the end.

Then I quickly tell the woman Teagan's room number, and she assures me she'll deliver it before I rush out the door to my patient.

I'D LIKE to say my mind is on my patient as I rush to the hospital. I'd like to say I can walk away from my night with Teagan without a second thought, like I have with several others throughout the past ten years. I'd like to say her leaving doesn't sting and wound my obviously inflated ego, if I thought last night was special for her as well.

I'd like to say those things—but that'd be a complete lie.

No, my memory goes into overdrive and recalls every minute detail of my night with Teagan. Every facial expression, every gasp, every moan. Nothing makes sense for why she'd suddenly disappear. We'd even made loose plans to spend another day together, since I didn't have to leave until tomorrow afternoon. Where the hell could she have gone?

Usually, driving clears my mind. But the entire route to Austin, my mind is on her. When I realize I've made the entire forty-minute drive without any recollection of how I got here, I chastise myself for being such a distracted driver. Parking my SUV in the physicians' lot, I quickly make my way to my locker.

The moment I walk through those doors, I force myself to compartmentalize.

It's what I do best. I have a four-year-old who needs my attention, and a team of people are counting on me. In a matter of weeks, I'll officially make the shift from resident to attending, and I feel with every fiber of my being, I'm ready to take on that challenge.

As soon as I change into scrubs to look less like I've just been on vacation, I meet Hannah at the nurses' station near the patient's room.

"Hi, Dr. Fallon. Welcome back. I hope you enjoyed your visit to Deacon."

She's the one who told me about the B&B and despite how things ended, I thoroughly enjoyed myself. "It was a much-needed break. Thanks for suggesting it."

"It's not much, but I enjoyed my trip there."

Not wanting my brain to linger on my activities in Deacon, I quickly prompt, "Bring me up to speed with this patient. While we walk to his room, is there anything out of the ordinary I need to know?"

As we turn to walk down the hall, Hannah prattles out the details. "Connor Frost, age four. Just had a birthday two weeks ago. He was visiting his grandparents for the week, and they took him to the park. There he played on the monkey bars and fell, resulting in a fractured olecranon. The fracture itself appears clean, but it could be problematic as it's near the growth plate. Based on the images, it will likely require surgery."

Knowing I can't go any further with a course of treatment without parental consent, I ask, "Have the parents been notified?"

"Yes. I believe they arrived about thirty minutes before you. They're all waiting for you."

Stopping at the door, I look to Hannah. "Thank you. Let's go meet Connor and see if we can put his family at ease."

From my experience with kids, they seem to trust you better if you confront them first. After knocking on the door to announce my arrival and giving ample time for a response, I swing the door open.

Immediately, my eyes go to the little boy lying in the large hospital bed. "Hi, Connor, I'm Dr. Fallon. I've heard you had an incident with the monkey bars. Let's see if we can get you fixed up."

Immediately, I notice his grandparents sitting in two chars off to the side, while his mother sits on the bed facing the boy, her back to me. The moment she turns her head, the wind is knocked out of me.

Holy shit. This can't be happening.

The same beautiful blue eyes I'd spent lost in last night stare back at me in shock.

Thankfully, I get a moment to recover because Hannah quickly takes this time to introduce herself. "I'm Dr. Brighton.

I'll be assisting Dr. Fallon. Would you mind letting us help fix your arm?"

Connor has the same expression as his mother. Shock and wariness loom over him as he squeezes his mom's hand. I can't imagine what's going through his head or how much pain he's been in, but I've been in this situation before, and I know in just a matter of days, he'll be acting like this never happened—despite the large cast he'll be toting.

Unlike some doctors, I find shooting straight with a touch of humor gets me a lot further than talking down to small children. Especially to break the ice. "I know you've seen a lot of doctors and nurses today and are probably pretty scared."

Connor's eyes widen as he silently nods once.

"It's okay to be scared. This is all new. But can I let you in on a little secret?" I ask conspiratorially as if no one can hear.

This piques his interest. His head tilts, and his brows lift.

"I'm not that scary. I don't even nibble on toes." I shrug as if that should explain everything. When his lips tilt into the slightest smile, I ask, "But I've heard you're quite the little monkey. Do I need to worry about you nibbling on my toes?"

Blinking as if he's unsure of what to say, I quickly add for reassurance, "I'm just teasing. But I've heard you're hurt. Want to tell me what's going on?"

Connor looks to his mom, and she nods in encouragement. "Tell Dr. Fallon what happened, sweetheart."

At first, I'm not sure he's going to say anything, but when Teagan squeezes his good hand in encouragement, Connor opens up. "I fell off da bars. First, I was swinging, then I fell and bonked my arm."

Knowing the doctors before me have already poked and prodded him, I try to keep my observations to a minimum. "Mind if I take a look?"

Connor nods in approval.

While tracing my fingers along his arm, I distract him with conversation. "From your shirt, I see you're a fan of *Paw Patrol*. I have lots of nieces and nephews who've watched that show. Do you have a favorite character?"

Nodding, Connor smiles for the first time. "All of dem. But I *love* Chase. Mommy lets me watch it if I'm up before we go to Frannie's."

"It's the only way I can get ready myself." Teagan chuckles, then admits to the room, "That's twenty-two precious minutes some days."

"No kidding," Hannah agrees. "You got to take every minute while you can."

The two of them continue talking, but I focus my attention on Connor. "I really like Rubble, as I loved to build things when I was your age."

"Really? Like what?"

"Hmmm... let's see... I built forts and all sorts of things. I grew up in the country, and I spent a lot of time outside."

"That's cool. I can only go outside if Mommy or a grown up comes, too." He shrugs, then winces slightly when his arm moves.

"That's a safe plan." Then I switch to the reason we're here. "Hey, Connor, can you count to ten?"

"Uh... Yeah." His eyes bug out like it's the stupidest question in the world.

"If one was little or no pain at all and ten is the worst you could ever imagine, where do you think you're feeling right this moment?" Holding up a card we use with younger patients that has different faces at each number, I watch him assess it carefully.

"A ten when I fell. But now dis." He points to a seven.

"What do you say we get you fixed up? I'll have to talk with your grown-ups, but after looking at your charts, I'm going to do everything I can to get you back to normal."

Connor nods but says nothing in return.

Turning to the adults in the room, I keep my language simple enough for Connor to understand. "As I'm sure you already know, he fractured his ulna." Looking to Connor, I add, "That bony part of your elbow."

"The good news is that it appears to be a clean break. However, it requires surgery to put it back in place."

Teagan looks warily at her son. "What will that entail?"

"The best course of treatment is to have an open reduction and an internal fixation to reset the bone. Basically, I'll need to go in and realign the bones to make sure they heal properly. I'll place temporary pins to hold it in place while he heals. Then when things look good, I'll remove them."

"Will there be permanent damage?" the other woman in the room asks.

"Given his age and type of fracture, I don't think so. There's always a chance it could affect his growth plate, but we won't know that until he continues growing. But most who've had this procedure return to normal within a couple of months. We'll monitor his progress every couple of weeks and when the final cast is off, he'll likely need some physical therapy to regain his strength and mobility."

"Since they live in Seattle, would it be best to have the surgery there?" the man who suddenly stands behind Teagan asks with concern.

"I wouldn't recommend traveling until the injury has been repaired, as it can cause unnecessary pain and possibly further injury. But if Ms. Frost is willing, I can follow up with Connor's surgery personally. I'm moving to Seattle and will be an attending physician at their children's hospital right about the time Connor will be due for a check-up."

Connor's grandfather just nods as Teagan's mouth drops.

His grandmother, oblivious to Teagan's reaction, says, "That's wonderful! Isn't it, Teagan?" Then she turns to me and asks, "Will they have any trouble flying home in a few days? Or should Teagan call the airlines and reschedule their flights now?"

"You're in luck once again," Hannah announces to the room. "We happen to have an open OR in just a few hours, and Dr. Fallon is available today. All we have to do is fill out the paperwork so that Ms. Frost can give her consent."

Before we go any further, I need to see if Teagan is on board with *me* being the one to perform surgery on her son. With everything that happened between us last night, I wouldn't blame her if she thought there is a conflict of interest.

Locking eyes with Teagan, worry fills her features. She's gnawing the hell out of her lower lip. Wanting to put her at ease, I'm dying to reach out and hug her—but that would be completely inappropriate. "Ms. Frost, would you mind if I speak to you outside so we can go over the specifics of the procedure?" Looking to Connor, I quickly add, "Don't worry, she'll be back in just a few minutes."

Teagan reaches out and brushes her son's hair from his face. "Will you be okay with Grandma and Grandpa for a minute?"

Connor looks from his mom to me as his grandma walks over and reaches for his good hand. "I'll be right here with you. Your momma needs to talk with the doctor. We'll be okay, won't we? I downloaded a *Paw Patrol* video on my phone just for you this morning."

"Really?" Connor perks up as he reaches for the phone she hands to him. Teagan is quickly forgotten.

His grandmother mouths, "Go," as Teagan looks from her to Connor.

Quietly, Teagan, Hannah, and I slip out of the room.

Once outside, I turn to Hannah. "Can you see where we are with the consent forms and make sure everything is set for surgery? I'll speak with Ms. Frost in the alcove near the nurses' station." Since it's protocol to never be alone, it'll be a private enough place to not be overheard, but still in public view.

"Sure. I'll also check on a patient of Dr. Jamison's to see if we're ready to discharge this evening."

"Sounds great."

The moment Hannah's out of earshot, my focus is entirely on Teagan's unreadable expression. Finally, when I can't take the silence any longer, I ask, "Can we talk?"

Chapter 8
Teagan

YES, we need to talk, but about what exactly? Our night of off the charts ecstasy, the fact that my son is injured and requires surgery, or the fact that he's the actual fucking surgeon—to which I had no clue of until he walked in the freaking door. Talk about adding further fuel to the fire on my level of stress.

As he stares into my eyes, holding me in place, he waits for an answer. As much as I know they're necessary, words won't form in my mouth, so I resort to what I can in this moment— a nod.

Once we're alone for the most part, he stops abruptly and steps into an empty waiting area. I swear he almost reaches for my hand, like he did so many times last night, but instead, he shoves them into his pockets. After a few moments of silence, he asks, "Are you okay?"

Knowing I'll never be anything less than honest with him, I admit, "I've had better days. Ever since that call this morning, I've been nothing but a ball of nerves and feeling so completely helpless, knowing there's nothing I can do for Connor to make him better."

"That's understandable," he agrees. "I don't want to add more stress to you, but I need to know—are you okay with me performing his surgery? If not, I'd recommend you keep with someone who specializes as a pediatric orthopedic surgeon. We're used to working with children and are better able to meet their needs as we routinely complete surgeries like this on small children. But If you'd rather it not be me, I'm sure I could get Dr. Jamison to return from paternity leave to complete this for you in a few days. After last night, I completely understand that you'd see this as a conflict of interest."

It takes me a moment to process his words.

"Waiting would mean Connor is in pain longer," I whisper. I can't do that to him.

"We can manage his pain with meds, so that won't be an issue." Davis counters before adding, "I just want to make sure you're comfortable with me performing surgery on your son."

"I'd be freaking out—no matter who's in there with him. Before you came, one of the emergency room doctors gave us the rundown of your experience and why they felt calling you in was considered their best call at this point. Given that Connor is so young, someone who specializes in pediatrics is a must—or so they said."

"That's true. I'm probably an even better choice than Jamison—not to sound full of myself—but at OHSU, I specialized in pediatric sports injuries and have actually completed this exact surgery more times than I would want to count, on both adults and children. But I never want you to feel as if you don't have a choice."

"I understand," I whisper. The thing is—Davis has done nothing to ever make me *not* trust him. "I just hate that my baby has to go through this. I seriously feel sick to my stomach and wish like hell I could take this pain from him."

"That's completely understandable. I can't even imagine how I'd feel as a parent in your shoes. But please know, he'd be in good hands with either Jamison or me. I'll do everything in my power to make sure he receives the best prognosis he can get."

Gnawing on my lower lip again, I finally ask my biggest concern, "How exactly would it work?"

"Miraculously, we don't have to wait long for an OR. In a few hours, we'd bring the two of you to a pre-op room. Here, a team of doctors will come and consult you individually, to walk you through their part of his surgery. The anesthesiologist will explain this more thoroughly, but essentially, they'll start Connor on an IV, and a nurse will help you prep for the surgery. You'll gown up and accompany Connor into the operating room."

"I have to watch you perform surgery?" I ask in disbelief. I may be brave at a lot of things, but I'm not sure I can handle watching my baby get cut open.

"Oh, no," Davis quickly rushes out. "When we're ready for surgery, we typically have the parent bring their child into the OR and wait for a matter of minutes for the anesthesiologist to give the patient a drug that knocks them out. Then you'll be escorted out, and we'll notify you when the surgery is over. In theory, it should take about an hour to complete. Then Connor will go to a recovery room and when he starts to wake up, we'll have you there ready to be with him."

"This is so much to process," I admit.

"I understand this can be scary, but Connor will be in good hands and as soon as you're able to, you'll be with him."

Taking a moment to process this wealth of information, another thought hits me. "Do you usually give such personal care to the parents of your patient?"

Without missing a beat, he pins me with his eyes. "Given our ... um circumstances..." He looks around before returning his focus to me. "I need to make sure you're completely on board with things before moving forward."

Sighing heavily, I weigh my options. "You need to perform the surgery. The sooner we get it done, the sooner Connor is back to normal."

Relief washes over Davis's beautiful face. "Thank you."

I'm not sure what he's thanking me for. Agreeing to the surgery or trusting him with my child's life.

"Will he need to stay in the hospital until we leave for Washington?"

"Oh, no," Davis quickly spits out again. "With any luck, you'll be discharged later this evening. But we may hold him overnight for observation—I won't be sure until the surgery is complete, so I don't want to give you misinformation."

Oh. Wow. That's soon. "Thank you so much for taking the time to explain everything to me, Davis. You can't imagine the stress I've been under to be in a strange place and my boy in pain."

"You're welcome, Teagan. If there's anything I can do to make this easier for you, just let me know."

Would he do this for all his patients' families? Or is this just how Davis is with me?

Before I can contemplate this further, Dr. Brighton returns. "Dr. Fallon, everything's set for surgery. Ms. Frost, when you're ready, a nurse will go over the necessary paperwork for us to get this show on the road. The surgery just got pushed up an hour, so a team of doctors will come through to explain everything in further detail shortly."

Holy shit. Everything's happening so fast.

Reaching out, Davis squeezes my shoulder for a long, calming moment. "Relax. We've got this. If you need anything, just let one of the nurses know, and it'll be taken care of. I'll see you when you bring Connor into the OR, and I'll be the one to come find you the moment it's done, to let you know how things went."

"Okay," I mutter as the crushing weight of what's to come suddenly overwhelms me.

Squeezing once more, he says, "Seriously, Ms. Frost. We've got this. It'll be over before we know it."

***

WATCHING my baby being put under is one of the hardest freaking things I've ever done. I can tell he wants to cry as he clings silently to me on the walk to the operating room. I'm dressed in paper scrubs, covered from head to toe, as I carry him into the room.

Looking at his little body lying on the table will forever be etched in my brain. I barely register Davis's reassurance that everything will be okay.

They'd better be. There's no way I can handle the loss of Connor.

No mother could.

This might be a minor procedure in the big scheme of things but having to sign my name on and read the potential hazards of this procedure, it brings on an entirely new set of fears I haven't even considered. Knowing he's never been put under, I have no idea how he'll react to the medications they're prescribing him.

Even though I've had support with me, in the form of Jacob's parents, it's not like I've ever been super close to them. I've tried keeping a brave face but when they said they were going to the cafeteria to grab something to eat, I can't make myself leave the room we've been left in to wait for Connor's recovery.

The moment the door shuts, and I'm alone, the dam of emotions I've been holding in bursts, and the tears I've been holding since finding out Connor is in the hospital stream down my face. His tiny little face, trying to look so brave, and his inflamed elbow is something that I will never forget. Since his birth, it's been Connor and me against the world. The thought of him undergoing something this scary alone guts me.

After I've given myself a moment to fall apart, I know I need to pull it together, or I'll be a blubbering mess when Connor returns, which of course will scare him even more. Grabbing some tissue from the box on the counter, I blot at my face. It won't do me any good to lose my shit. Connor needs me to be stronger than this for him.

Needing to wash my face, I walk to the bathroom nearby and take a moment to scrub away my tears. Catching my reflection in the mirror, I realize I'm a hot mess. I likely still smell of Davis, and I haven't brushed my teeth or my hair, and I'd give just about anything to take a long, hot bath. My messy bun is falling to the side as wisps of hair flow around my face. I'm still wearing my dress from yesterday, and I'm certain my deodorant has expired.

Fuck, all my clothes are still at the bed and breakfast.

I hadn't even thought to pack.

I just rushed out of there like the world was ending—which in a way it was, and I didn't give it a second glance. That means no matter what time we get out of here, I'll have nearly an hour drive to retrieve my things. I'm sure Jim and Dianne will be okay with Connor and me staying at Tilly's tonight, though they've asked I stay the remainder of this trip with them. We can return to their place in the morning. If for some reason Connor is admitted tonight, I'll just run to the store to get a change of clothes and some essentials.

Walking back to the waiting room, I'm relieved to find it empty. I could use a few more moments to myself. I attempt to distract myself by scrolling aimlessly through all my social media apps. After what seems like forever, I look at the time, and I'm devastated to realize Connor's only been in surgery for about thirty minutes.

This is the longest fucking hour of my life.

Sitting in the reclining chair, I will myself to relax. I close my eyes and try to focus on the sounds around me rather than the thoughts twirling around like a tornado in my head. With the door cracked open so the Harringtons will be free to enter, I listen to footsteps approaching and continuing down the hall. I hear the faint sound of a heart monitor in a room nearby, and I hear laughter coming from the nurses' station. All the while, I count my steady breaths flowing in for two, three, four, five seconds and out just as slow. It's not effective, but I'm no longer losing my shit, so I guess this diversion is better than nothing.

When there's a light knock on the door, I nearly bolt from the chair.

Seeing Davis's triumphant smile instantly sets my racing heart at ease. "Sorry to startle you, but the door was open. I came as soon as I could to tell you the news."

"No... that's okay. I've been going out of my mind waiting," I mutter as I close the distance between us. "Please tell me he's okay," I practically beg.

Nodding profusely, he grins from ear to ear. "Everything went as planned. Connor's break was clean, and I was able to get it repositioned and stabilized with only three pins. Everything's in a cast so you won't have to worry about him bumping anything when his energy returns to normal."

"Oh my God. Thank you, Davis!" I throw my arms around him.

Wrapping his arms around me, he pulls me close. "You're welcome, T. I'm glad I was able to help. With any luck, Connor will be as good as new in no time. Of course, we'll have to see how he feels after he comes out of recovery, but he should be released this evening."

I keep replaying the words he's just told me in my head as if I'm unsure they're real. Still clinging to him, I pull back to look him in the eye. "He's really gonna be okay?"

With another tight hug, I feel a kiss to the top of my head. "Yes. He really is. The better question is, are you?"

"I will—I just need to see him for myself, if you know what I mean."

I feel the rumble of laughter more than hear it through Davis's chest. "I can only imagine. But he really is okay. I saw with my own eyes."

Squeezing him once more, I say, "Thank you for giving Connor a chance to heal properly. I'm sure it will take awhile to recover, but I'll be forever grateful for you fixing him."

"I'm glad Jamison's boy chose today to be born—so I could."

Pulling back, Davis locks his gaze on mine for an immeasurable moment. Somehow, in all this chaos, our chemistry from last night soars back to life, and I find myself thinking of kissing him to show my appreciation.

He must feel it, too, as he slowly leans in to close the distance.

Before our lips can connect, a loud shrill from his phone fills the room, making us jump apart.

"Shit. That's my service. I have to take this."

Thinking it might be about Connor, I quickly step away as he says, "This is Davis Fallon." He listens for a moment as his eyes pinch together with concentration. "I'll be right there. Get an OR ready and have Brighton join me."

The minute he ends his call, his apologetic face says it all. "There's been a vehicular accident involving a bus filled with teens and a semi-truck. There are multiple open fractures, which means I'm busy for the foreseeable future. Please know Connor is in good hands, but I won't be able to see him before he discharges this evening. Who knows how many cases I'll have tonight. A nurse will reach out to schedule a follow-up appointment in Seattle from their children's hospital. I've already put in the orders."

He reaches out to squeeze my hand, then turns and rushes out of the room.

Before I can even process a word he's said, Dianne and Jim return and point down the hall in the direction Davis went.

"Was that the doctor?" Dianne asks.

I go through the motions of telling them that Connor's in recovery and that the surgery went as well as expected. Their bodies sag with relief, and they each take turns hugging me. They may only see Connor a few times a year, but I know without a doubt, they love him just as much as I do.

Eventually, a nurse comes to tell us that Connor's starting to wake up and that I can go see him. I almost want to hug her, too, for not making me wait much longer. I swear I've aged ten years in the span of the last few hours, and I'm not sure my nerves can handle waiting to see him much longer.

When I reach the curtained-off bed, the weight I didn't know I'd been carrying lifts the moment my beautiful boy opens his beautiful blue eyes and asks, "Is it over, Mommy?"

Rushing to close the distance between us, I lean in and carefully run my palm against his cheek. "Yes, sweet boy. I just spoke with Dr. Fallon, and he said you're gonna be okay."

Leaning in, I kiss his forehead as I whisper, "I love you so, so much."

Even though his voice is groggy, his words slay me. "I love you more, Mommy."

And just like that—being able to touch my son and see he's okay set my world right again.

Chapter 9
Davis

I'VE BEEN STARING at this screen for the past hour. I'm supposed to be catching up on my charts, but the moment I click on Connor Frost's file, my eyes have been glued to his emergency contact number. My thumb itches to swipe open my phone and call Teagan. I'm certain she's due to leave tomorrow, but it could have been today.

Either way, if she'd wanted to reach out to me, she would have, right?

I didn't think to ask for her number. Hell, both times, we've never had the chance to say goodbye. No, each time, emergencies have taken us away. As much as it was a shock to see her again, I'm glad to know the reason she left so abruptly.

I could just call her—it's right here.

But that would violate her privacy.

I've already crossed into the murky gray area due to our prior relations and not disclosing it with anyone. Snagging her number for personal use would just keep that line further blurred.

No. I shouldn't do this.

She clearly hasn't wanted to reach out, and I should just take that as a sign that whatever went on between us is over.

But why am I still staring at those ten measly digits?

Of course, I've already memorized them, but I'm not sure I should use them.

I'm not used to getting a girl's number—so it didn't even occur to me that I'd want it later. We knew the stakes—we had a few days. Then it's back to my life at the hospital, and she'd be whatever she does regularly.

So why can't I stop thinking about her?

Not only hasn't she reached out, but she's a single mom. That thought alone makes me pause.

All my memories suddenly take on new meaning, knowing the real reason she's put her own needs on the back burner. I'm certain it's because she's always a mom first. Which of course is how it should be. I still don't know her backstory, or whether Connor's dad is in the picture, and maybe I'll never know. But I can't for the life of me, stop thinking about her.

I should just close the chart and forget about her. It's not like things between us can go anywhere. I'm starting a new job, and she has her son to think of. I'm sure I'm the last thing on her mind now that they're heading back to Seattle.

"Hey, stranger," brings me back to reality.

It's Caitlyn, a fellow nurse and a woman I've hooked up with occasionally since arriving in Austin. It started out as friends and turned to friends with benefits when neither of us are seeing anyone else. But neither of us caught feelings or have any expectations for the other.

She doesn't wait for me to respond. "Wanna grab a beer tonight and hang out?"

She and I both know hanging out typically leads to us ending up in bed, but what once was a mutually satisfying venture, doesn't even interest me. It has nothing to do with her being undesirable—I'm just not in the right head space.

"Nah, I have to finish these charts. With only another few weeks left here, I can't get behind." By her cringe, I can tell something's on her mind. "What's up?"

With a playful smile, she shrugs. "I wanted to butter you up to ask for a favor. One of my good friends is about to lose her fig orchard, and we're making a calendar. One of the guys backed out and..." She crinkles her nose but doesn't continue.

This uncertainty is completely out of character for Caitlyn, so I can't figure out why she's suddenly acting weird. "What does this have to do with me?"

"I was kinda hoping I could talk you into filling in for him."

"Uh... why would anyone want a photo of me? They don't even know me."

Her eyes roll to the back of her head as she sighs with disapproval. "Davis..." she says pointedly, "have you bothered to look in a mirror lately?"

"Now you're just being ridiculous," I guffaw. She's clearly out of her mind if she thinks I'd be interested in doing something like this.

"Seriously, Davis, I need your help. This is important. My friend, Tricia, is freaking out that she won't be able to save an orchard that's been in her family for years. They're on a tight timeline, and this calendar is a way to get the funds quickly.

It's in serious need of repair. You know I never ask for favors. And I'll owe you big time if you can help me out."

She pins me with pleading eyes, and I do my best to ignore them as I remind her, "You do know I'm leaving soon, right?"

"The shoot is next week, and it should only take a few hours of your time."

Well, shit. She has me there.

"It's basically a charity—you're always running 10Ks and whatnot for other organizations. This won't even require training. You just show up, take a few pictures, and you'll never have to see anyone again."

"Caitlyn..." I draw out in a groan. "Don't you have someone else you could ask?"

Smirking, she shakes her head. "No one as hot as you."

"Now you're just lying... isn't that beneath you?"

"Seriously, Davis, I'm desperate. I'll even grab your favorite coffee on my way in to work from now until the day you leave. I know you can't resist their homemade pastries."

She lives next to the best unknown coffee shop I've found since leaving Washington. There's never a long line, and their daily treats are made fresh locally right there in the shop. It's entirely out of my way, but I've been known to treat myself more often than I'd like to admit.

She senses my firm line is cracking. "You know we're on the same shifts for the next two weeks... That's two whole weeks of not having to drive out of your way.

"All I'm asking for is a few hours of your time. The photo shoot will be in Deacon, and it'll be over before you know it."

The thought of delicious coffee and pastries each morning

is amazing... but doing a photo shoot—that's just not my thing. She puts her hands together in prayer and gives me the biggest puppy dog eyes I've ever seen. She even sticks out her lower lip in the most pathetic pout possible. She must be desperate. "Ugh.... Why are you doing this to me?"

"Because the ladies will love Dr. Fallon." Her words roll off her tongue as her face morphs into a triumphant smile.

"As long as *no* personal information is attached to it. I don't want to be tagged on social media—not that I do much of that, but my family will give me hell for this. God knows the fiasco Dani and Luke went through when he was mistaken as one of her cover models. It was a PR nightmare for both of them."

"Deacon's a small town, Davis. I'm sure the only ones appreciating your generosity will be its town members."

Sighing heavily, I give her the words she's anxiously been waiting for. "Okay... but I'd better not regret this."

Leaning in, she kisses me on the cheek. "You are a gem, Dr. Fallon. Don't worry; that will be the only personal information they'll get out of me."

Did I just say I'd model for her?

"If you're busy tonight, do you want to catch up before you leave?"

It's been a couple of months since we've used the *benefits* part of our friendship. She started dating someone for a couple of weeks, but it didn't work out between them. Our schedules have just never meshed since. But now, my head's not in it. Since we've always been honest with one another, I'm not stopping now.

"I, uh... met someone while I was in Deacon."

"Really, anyone I know?" She's from there. Of course, she'd ask that.

"No. She's not from here. I'm certain it'll never go anywhere, but I'm not in the headspace to be even casual with you when I haven't stopped thinking about her."

Apparently unfazed by my news, she smiles. "No worries, I completely understand. We're still getting drinks with the gang before you leave though. There's no way you're getting out of the going away party Becks and I have planned."

Jordan Becks is another resident I've become friends with since arriving in Austin. He's a great guy, and it's been nice to have someone to commiserate with as we navigate this residency. We all started around the same time at the hospital, and after some shared traumas, we have bonded easily. "I wouldn't miss it."

"Good." She smiles triumphantly. "I've gotta go make a call and tell Tricia. We have all twelve models, and this shoot is a go."

What the hell have I just gotten myself into?

Shaking my head, my focus returns to the screen.

Teagan, you have me completely discombobulated and for the first time in forever, I don't know what the right move is.

I guess I'll just have to wait to see what happens when I see you in Seattle.

And with that, I close the file and will myself to walk away from the computer.

Chapter 10
Teagan

WE'VE BEEN HOME from Texas for almost three weeks. Thank God, Connor's a trooper. Other than the fact he sometimes needs help because he doesn't have two hands, you'd hardly know his arm is in a full cast and sling. Davis was right, I'm more traumatized than Connor over this entire ordeal.

Now that I've returned to work after my rollercoaster vacation, I'm looking forward to an evening with my best friend Annie. Mom has Connor for the night for some "grandma time." It's something they do at least once a month. She drives down from Everett to spend the weekend with us. She used to blatantly kick me out of my house so I would enjoy some time for myself or time with friends. She knows being a single mom is hard and wants to make sure I get a break from time to time. Besides—it's her way of spoiling her only grandchild in the process—so as she says, it's a win-win.

Tonight, I'm meeting Annie at a bar down the street from her office. She recently ventured out on her own and opened her new advertising business. I only know a fraction of what she does on a daily basis—as I've developed and designed her website. But I know it's been a hell of a lot of work. I'm certain she'll kick ass, like she always does. She's taken on more clients and has even had to hire additional help to keep up with things. I'm so freaking proud of her. But like me, she desperately needs a night out to unwind. I can't wait to finally catch up with her in person.

When I walk in, I find her at our favorite high-top table close to the stage and dance floor. Tonight's Karaoke Night and after a few drinks, I'm certain we'll be belting our favorite songs from our youth or at the very least, shaking our ass on the dance floor to others smashing it.

When she sees me, she stands and wraps me in a hug. "Teagan, I'm so glad to see you. I've missed you so much!"

"It's only been a few weeks, Annie. It's not like we don't talk daily."

Shaking her head, she disagrees. "Not the same. I feel terrible that I haven't been able to check on Connor yet."

She had to fly to Vegas to meet with a potential client. While she was there, she took a few days to travel to Palm Springs to visit her grandmother.

"You've seen him on video chats and talk to both of us daily. Don't sound too put out. Besides, I'm not the one putting in long hours with Nate and been too busy to stop by," I tease.

Nate Bellinger was Annie's first hire when she realized in order to expand, she needed additional help. He'd worked with her at Meyer & Cross, and she's always had a bit of a crush on him. This tiny fact was almost the reason she didn't consider hiring him. But his record and potential clients alone, were worth putting her thoughts about him aside. She swears she only views him professionally, but it doesn't mean I don't tease her about it. I mean—what else are best friends for?

"You know it's not like that," she chastises. "He's my employee, and I'm not going there."

"Okay…" I draw out exaggeratedly. "If you say so. But you and I both know I'm not buying it."

Shaking her head, she sighs heavily. "Whatever you say, crazy pants."

Before either of us can say anything, Tara, our favorite waitress, stops by. "Hey, ladies, long time no see. What can I get for you tonight?"

Each of us orders some appetizers and drinks from the happy hour menu without even looking at it, and Tara rushes off.

When someone starts singing, "Single Ladies," by Beyoncé, the crowd buzzes with energy as they join in. When Annie raises a brow in my direction, we jump to our feet and start the choreographed moves from her video to match the crowd. This is a favorite of mine growing up and one I will always dance to.

By the time the song is over, Tara's brought our drinks to our table. "Your steak bites and spinach dip will be out in a minute. Need anything else?"

Annie reaches for her Moscow Mule. "Nope, Tara, we're good. Thank you."

Taking a sip of my mojito, I exhale heavily and release the tension from the day. This new program I'm writing is challenging in a fun sort of way, but at the moment, I just want my mind to turn to mush and relax.

Not having to rush out the door to pick up Connor from Frannie's is huge. Frannie is the woman who watches Connor in her in-home daycare. I got lucky when I found her because Connor just thrives with her. She has a grandchild of her own and two others Connor's age who spend the day together while I'm at work. Thank God, Mom took that responsibility off my plate today. I love my child, but I deserve this break, too.

For a moment, we watch the next singers as the beats to "Uptown Funk" fill the room. He's impressive and sounds as if Bruno himself is here singing to us. He's highly entertaining. When our food arrives, my attention quickly turns to that.

"God, I'm starving," I admit as I scoop the creamy artichoke dip with a chip and lift it to my mouth. "I got so engrossed in code that I forgot to eat my lunch. It didn't even faze me until my stomach rumbled on the way over."

"Only you could *forget* to eat. What are you working on now?"

"I'm developing an app for a client to help her streamline her POS processing. She's been able to use other systems, but when I'm done, she'll have customized features that combine the best features from multiple apps she currently uses, for both her eCommerce and shop, from the touch of a button."

"Wow... I have no idea what that even means, but you certainly sound excited about it, and I'm happy for you, my brilliant friend." Yeah, I'm far more of a techie than Annie needs. She loves technology and uses many apps herself regularly, but as she often jokes, she just wants the end product, not to see how the sausage is made, so to say.

"I am. It's exciting to help others build their business efficiently."

"I get that. Did I tell you I heard from that potential client in Vegas? They have narrowed it down to two agencies. Nate and I are flying back down together to put together another pitch. The client claims to be forward thinking but is a bit old school when it comes to seeing the presentations in person, rather than virtual meetings. If we get this account, it could put me about three years ahead of my plan for expansion."

"Holy shit, that's incredible. You and Nate work so well together, so I'm certain you'll be able to pull it off."

"I have a great plan, but it'll take a lot to pull it off. Either way—that's not tonight's worry." Just as she says this, Ed Sheeran's "Shape of You" starts. The energy in the room shifts, and I find myself swaying to the music in my seat.

God, I love this song. I'm so focused on the man slaying his performance, that I don't even notice when another man approaches our table. It isn't until he's directly standing between me and my view of the stage that I even know he's there.

Locking eyes on me, he smiles lazily. "I can't help but notice you like this song; wanna dance?" He's tall with dark, wavy hair that curls at the ends. The kind of hair I'd usually want to run my hands through. But even though he's handsome, I'm just not feeling it.

"Thanks, but I'm here to catch up with a friend, and we just got our food." I point to my chip now covered with dip again, then to Annie, whose expression says a million words yet remains silent.

"That's totally understandable. Enjoy your evening." And he's gone as quick as he arrived.

I fork a piece of steak and slowly enjoy its savory flavor. I could eat these every day for the rest of my life, and I don't think I'll ever tire.

Then I notice Annie still staring at me.

"What?" I ask defensively. "Did I spill something on me?"

Tilting her head to get a better angle at whatever she's looking at, her jaw pops open, then slowly closes, making me feel even more self-conscious.

What the hell is wrong with her?

Finally, she breaks her silence. "Since when do you not dance to your favorite song?"

Shrugging, I remind her, "I told you I was hungry."

"Hmmm..." She nods suspiciously, then goes in for the kill. "So... have you heard from your dreamy Doctor Davis?"

"Uh, last I checked, I'm not on *Grey's Anatomy*—and who uses the word dreamy? Are you suddenly sixty? I'm pretty sure I would've told you, since we talk every day, but no, I haven't heard from him. Besides, he has my number. He obviously didn't want to reach out."

"You gave him your number?" she asks in confusion. "You never told me that."

"Well, I gave it to the nurse at the hospital. Clearly, he doesn't want to see me again."

Pity flashes across her features, and confusion fills mine. "Teagan. You may be the smartest person I know, but you are so dumb sometimes. The nurse will only use that number to call you during the surgery. He likely will never see the number."

Shit, I never thought of that.

"Clearly, you're not over him if you won't even dance with another guy."

"Of course, I'm not over him. We had one perfect day, but I'm sure that'll be all it ever amounts to. I'll look at the photos and replay that night in my dreams when I sleep for many months to come. He's single and carefree, and I'm a single mom who can't put her needs first. But I won't lie to myself and say I don't miss the way he could read my body like he was given a special-coded map, or the way I was able to trust him implicitly after just meeting him."

I remember every kiss, every touch, and more importantly, the way he could wring Os out of me like it was his personal mission in life. Yeah, it's best to keep my trusty vibrator charged, replaying that night on a loop is about all the action I'll be getting for the inevitable future.

"Connor's appointment is tomorrow, right?" Annie asks, breaking me from my tangled thoughts.

"Yeah." The thought alone of seeing Davis again sends shivers up my spine.

"Girl—you've got it bad."

"It's not like that," I insist. "I'm nervous about Connor's prognosis. He's been rambunctious lately, and I worry they'll have to go through all that again to reset the bone or something will go wrong." All these thoughts are honestly my fears, though thoughts of Davis are at times more predominant.

God, I do have it bad.

"I'm sure that's true—but sell it to someone else, sister— you want to see him."

Sighing heavily, I admit my feelings. "Yeah, but it's not like anything can come of it."

"I'm not so sure."

I guess I'll just have to see, won't I... That thought alone scares the shit out of me.

———

TAKING CONNOR'S HAND, we walk through the hospital doors. He goes from being his usual chatty self, to unusually quiet. Hopefully, he's just taking in the enormous mural of the ocean on the wall, rather than getting scared again. We had a conversation last night and this morning about how the worst is behind us. He just has to have patience and most importantly —let his arm heal.

When we check in, I have more paperwork to fill out— since this is his first visit to this hospital. Just as I'm finishing it, the nurse calls Connor's name.

The moment we stand, a woman about my mother's age walks to greet us. "Hi, Connor, I'm Miss Carol. I'm going to help you get ready to see Dr. Fallon. Right this way."

She leads us down the hall and around the corner to an exam room. "Here we go. Have there been any problems since your surgery?"

I look to Connor who just shrugs. "I don't think so."

"That's great. We're going to change out your cast today. By now, the swelling has likely gone down, and your arm is likely smaller than it was right after surgery—not to mention, it might be kinda stinky." With that, she makes a face, and Connor laughs. "You're going to meet with Dr. Fallon, and he'll explain how your exam will go, then I'll take you to the casting room."

She types a few things into the computer in the exam room and by the time she's done, there's a knock on the door. My spine tingles, and the energy shifts in the room. Davis's eyes find mine instantly, and I can't believe he's even better looking than I remember.

When I saw him last, he was clean shaven. Now he has a few days' growth on his handsome face, which makes his brown eyes pop. It's not scruff, but it's not a full beard either. I'm normally not one for facial hair, but Davis pulls it off with ease.

My eyes never leave him as he greets my son with ease. "Hey, Connor. It's great to see you again. Has your arm been hurting at all?"

"No, but it gets itchy."

"We'll see what we can do about getting you a different cast, which should be lighter since it won't have to be as thick to keep your arm in place."

"Can I get a blue cast, like Chase?"

"Absolutely." Davis smiles. Then he turns his attention to me. "Did Miss Carol tell you what's going to happen today?"

"Just that we'll take the cast off."

Davis nods. Then he bends down to get to Connor's eye level. "Hey, buddy?"

"Yeah?"

"We're going to take your cast off with a machine that sounds loud and will make your arm vibrate. But don't worry, it won't cut you, okay?"

Connor nods in understanding.

"When it gets off, your arm will look kind of different. It may still have some bruises, and there will be some pins keeping it in place. Can you try hard not to straighten your arm?"

Connor just nods.

"Your mom will stay with you until it's time for your x-ray. Then Miss Carol will take you to get a picture of your arm."

Focusing his attention on me, he flashes that sexy smile that could melt my panties in an instant. "Do you have any questions?"

"No. I'm good."

"Let's take you to the casting room then."

Miss Carol leads the way as Davis holds the door for us. Like always, when he's in a new situation, Connor takes my hand to go down the hall. Walking past Davis, his faint cologne floods my brain with memories of our night together. It's as if I've been transported back to Texas, and it takes a lot of strength to not reach out to touch him.

The casting room has multiple patient beds. There's a teenage girl getting a new cast on her arm and a boy not much older than Connor getting one cut off his foot.

Davis must notice Connor's posture stiffen because the minute Connor sits on the patient bed, he gets to his eye level to comfort him. "Don't worry, Connor. I can stay with you the entire time you get the cast cut off if you'd like. It sounds much worse than it is, trust me."

Then he walks over to the counter and grabs some gloves to put on. Grabbing a piece of cast from the trash beside him, he walks over and says, "Watch this." He pulls over a saw similar to the one being used on the bed across the room. "See. Touch the top. All it does is vibrate. The blade itself barely extends beyond the guard."

With Connor placing a finger on the cast in Davis's hands, Davis presses the button on the saw and cuts into the other end of it for a second or two. When the machine turns off, Connor giggles. "That tickles."

"Yep." Davis nods in agreement. "That's how it's going to feel. I'll cut along here." He draws a finger up both the left and right of Connor's arm. "Then I will have to use a special tool to split the cast apart entirely. I may even need to cut some of the bandages. Okay?"

My heart pings at the way he takes the time to explain this to Connor. He could have easily had a nurse or someone else do the task. I'm sure he's busy, but right now, it's as if we're his only patients for the day.

Within a few minutes, the cast is removed, and Connor's arm is exposed. I know I'll likely regret it, but I look at the wound. There's still ink from the surgery written on my son's tiny arm and three thin metal rods sticking out. Instead of being straight, they're curved at the ends. It looks gross, but not as bad as I'd imagined a million times in my mind.

He takes a few minutes to clean up Connor's hand and forearm with a damp cloth. When he's done, he looks to me.

Miss Carol approaches with a wheelchair and says, "I'm not taking any chances with you, mister. Wanna go for a ride to x-ray?"

As soon as Connor's settled, Davis pats him on his good shoulder. "I'll meet you in the exam room, and we'll look at the picture of your arm together."

Davis nods once in my direction and takes off with a chart in his hands.

I walk with Carol and Connor to x-ray. There's one person ahead of him, so Miss Carol suggests, "You're welcome to wait for us in the exam room. It's the second door on the right."

When another person passes us in the narrow hall, I realize there isn't a lot of room for me here, and I'm basically just in the way. Leaning down, I kiss the top of Connor's head. "I'll see you in a few minutes, sweet boy. You be good for Miss Carol."

"Don't you worry." She looks conspiratorially to Connor. "I won't pop too many wheelies on the way back," which causes him to giggle adorably.

The x-ray room door opens, and a patient and a nurse exit.

"We're up, Connor. Are you ready to find out if your bones are healing?"

And that's my cue to leave.

I'm not nearly as emotional as I was before, but it's not easy putting on a brave face for Connor. It'll be good to just take a moment to myself while I wait for Connor to return. The door to the exam room is cracked open. When I walk in, I'm surprised to find I'm not alone.

Davis leans against the counter. His long legs stretch out

with one crossed over while his arms cross over his broad chest. His sexy lips lift in a smile as he watches me enter. Just one look has my heart fluttering out of control.

"I hope you don't mind, but I thought we could talk while we wait for Connor to return."

This can go one of two ways and with his unreadable expression, I'm not sure which way. Part of me wants to walk right into his arms, the other—bolt out the door.

Instead, I do neither and find myself standing just inside the door saying, "That's fine."

His voice is low when he takes a step closer to me and shuts the door behind me.

As much as I wish he'd touch me, he doesn't. But the look in his eyes tell me he wants to. Taking a long breath, Davis sighs heavily. "God, why does it feel like forever since I've last seen you? These have been the longest four weeks of my life—I swear."

"Same," I whisper.

I want to reach for him, but when he stuffs his hands into his pockets, I think better of it.

He looks to the floor briefly, then back to my eyes. "I'll never be anything less than honest with you, Teagan."

"Okay," I draw out, wondering where he's going with this.

"I haven't stopped thinking about you, and I'd really like to see you again."

"Same."

Great, now I sound like I can only say one syllable responses.

Reaching out, he caresses my cheek as he brushes a loose

strand of hair behind my ear. Then he shakes his head and sighs. "But I can't do anything because Connor's my patient. His surgery was pretty intensive, and I'd prefer not to hand this case over to anyone else. Not only is he your child, but I want to make damn certain I've done everything I can for him as my patient."

I want what's best for my son, but my heart sinks at the thought of not being able to see Davis again.

"With me just starting at this hospital, I can't cross any lines—not that I would otherwise. But our situation is unique."

"Yes, it is," I agree.

Neither of us say anything as we stare into each other's eyes for a long minute.

Eventually, he clears his throat and asks, "Can I make you a deal?"

"What's that?" I counter.

What could he possibly want?

"Can I continue being Connor's physician? Then when he's no longer my patient, if we still feel the same way as I think we do, can I take you out?"

Relief floods through me knowing I'm not alone in this after all. As the realization hits, I feel a smile spread across my face. "I think I can handle that." Everything in my being wants to spring into his arms, but we're at his place of work. I keep myself firmly rooted in place.

Running a hand through his hair, he looks to the sky. "Depending on how the x-ray comes back, it could be another four to six weeks of waiting."

Please let it be four weeks.

Not only would it mean Connor is out of his cast, but selfishly, the thought of another night with Davis like we had in Deacon makes my libido roar wildly.

She is definitely on board with that plan.

Before either of us can say a word, there's a light knock on the door. "Guess who was a trooper?"

Connor greets me with glee. "Mommy, look! I got a new stuffy for being good."

Sure enough, he's cuddling an adorable brown and white dog.

"I'm so proud of you for being a sweet boy without me. It was nice of Miss Carol to give you that. Did you thank her?"

Rolling his eyes, he shakes his head. "Yes, Mommy."

God help me when he's a teen.

Davis taps on the computer, and the monitor springs to life. "Let's take a look at those images and see what you look like from the inside out."

"Cool. Will I see those poky things in there?"

"Yep. There they are. And right there..." He points to the tip of the elbow. "Is where you're healing. When you come back next time, that little line will practically disappear."

To me, Davis says, "He's healing as expected. If all goes well, he'll get the pins out in about four weeks. We'll determine then if he'll need a cast or can start physical therapy to regain mobility. Until then, just try to stay off the monkey bars and out of trees."

"Duh... I can't climb with one hand. I need dem both. I'm *not* a superhero."

Chuckling, Davis pats Connor on the shoulder. "Well, be nice to your mom and try to take it easy. Can you do that?"

Connor nods eagerly.

"Let's get you back to that cast room and get a cast the color of Chase for you." Then Davis turns to me and pulls a card from his pocket. "If you need anything between now and our next visit, just give me a call, and we'll have you come in earlier."

I'm sure he gives every patient's parent his card, but when his hand grazes mine, heat floods through me, and I crave more. Before I can make a scene, I shove the card in my pocket and follow him back to the cast room.

It isn't until I get home that I find the note he'd written on the back:

Hope I hear from you soon!
P.S. This is my personal number
~ D

Holy shit. He wrote this before he even knew what I'd say today.

Chapter 11
Davis

IT'S NEARLY seven by the time I get home that evening. Though home is a loose term, as I'm technically staying at my oldest brother Derek's. Yes, he and his wife just had a baby, but they have a place in Bear Creek, Colorado, and they're spending the next month or so in Colorado. They're visiting her dad and a few friends, as well as checking in on her brewery. Hopefully, they'll travel less once she opens another brewery here in Seattle.

I seriously doubt Tessa will take more than six weeks off for maternity leave. Derek's doing his damnedest to make sure she rests. I know she won't overdo it, but it's a good thing he can work from anywhere with his graphic design business—to keep her from working herself to death once her six weeks are up. I'm not sure of their actual plans for living arrangements once the new brewery opens here in Seattle, but their empty house allows me not to rush looking for a place of my own.

Before they left, I got to make sure Melody spent time with her favorite uncle for a few days. I was glad to help for a few hours because Derek and Tessa were beyond exhausted being new parents. I swear the moment they realized she was snuggled with her favorite blanket and fast asleep on my chest, they snuck out of the room to nap themselves. I, too, got to enjoy my gift and of course—deemed myself as the favorite uncle once again.

Tonight, I grabbed dinner on my way home from the hospital, so I plop down on the couch to watch *SportsCenter*. With football season underway, I like to get the highlights of what I've missed this week. The Renegades had back-to-back games on the road, so I haven't seen Dani or Luke since returning to Seattle. Her kids aren't in school yet and since one of the games was against Tennessee, she took them to visit Luke's parents. I don't think I'd want to travel with two kids five and under, but she claims they're experts, and my mom and dad went with her to help.

Kicking my shoes off, I rest my feet on the ottoman.

When my phone rings, I scramble to dig it out of my pocket.

Please let it be Teagan.

I gave her my card hours ago, but I haven't heard anything.

Nope—just my brother Damien.

"Hey, Dame, what's up?"

"I should be asking you, shouldn't I? Are you liking the fact that as an attending, you no longer have to work the grunt hours at the hospital?"

"It's a change, that's for sure. I think it will be nice to be able to schedule time away from the hospital each day. Hell, I only work one weekend a month, so I can't complain."

"No, you've earned it, man. You've worked your ass off since school. I would have given up years ago—so you're a better man than me. I was happy to get out of school with my master's degree."

"I'm only twenty-eight... so I took the long route," I tease. I know he's proud of me, but it's been a running joke that I'd never be out of school for years. As a pediatric orthopedic surgeon, it was bound to take longer than most to specialize in my field.

"Will we see you at the game in two weeks?"

"Yep! I can't wait to see Jules and the twins." His boys just turned four and keep him and Vanessa on their toes. Vanessa and Dame handle it like pros—though with Jules being nearly six years older, she's a huge help.

"Jasper and Jordan will be higher than kites to see you. They're already talking about piggyback rides and ice cream— watch out."

"How else will I stay their favorite uncle? Vince may see them most, but they know who's number one."

"It's a good thing you don't have an ego or anything."

When an unknown number rings in and flashes across my screen, I make my excuse to get off. "Listen, man, I have another call. I'll catch up with you later."

"This is Davis Fallon," I say out of habit.

"Well, hello to you, Davis Fallon. If we're being formal, it's me—Teagan Frost. Is this a bad time?"

My heart pounds in my chest as relief of finally hearing her voice flows through me. "No. I just got home. How are you doing?"

"Well… is it bad I couldn't wait for Connor's bedtime to call you?"

"You have no idea how long I've been wanting to hear your voice," I admit. "I've been kicking myself for weeks that I didn't get your number."

"I felt so bad leaving so abruptly."

"Teagan—Connor will always come first. Though I guess I should thank Jamison because without his wife going into labor, I wouldn't have seen you again."

Her beautiful laughter comes through the phone. "I hadn't thought of that. I was so stuck in my head, I couldn't see beyond getting Connor the help he needed."

"I'm glad it all worked out."

Needing to change the subject, I try to think of something to say. "Uh… I just realized we missed a few steps when we met in Deacon. Maybe this moratorium on dating will make it so we can back up and get to know one another."

"That's one way to look at it." I can hear the smile in her voice when she adds, "I'm Teagan Renee Frost. I'll be twenty-five in March. I'm a software developer—and sometimes my inner nerd shows. I don't get a lot of free time because I have an adorable four-year-old who's smart, witty, and adventurous."

"March what?"

"Thirteenth. What's your story? I just gave you the dime version, so you can do the same."

I certainly hope I get to know her much better than a dime's worth. "Let's see… I'm twenty-eight, apart from living in Austin for the past two years, I've also lived in Washington my entire life—though I did a short stint in Portland when I attended school at OHSU. You already know I'm the youngest of four, and I am the proud uncle to six nieces and nephews. I take that job seriously as I have to compete with my brothers, Luke, and Vanessa's brother Vince."

"I can tell you're not competitive at all," she teases.

"Guilty. What about you—do you have siblings?"

"Nope. I'm an only child, and my parents live in Everett."

We talk for the next two hours, and I learn about how she fell in love with computers in middle school and has been a self-proclaimed nerd ever since.

When it creeps past midnight, she gasps. "I have to be up in five hours. I'd better get going."

"Can I call you tomorrow?"

"You'd better. Night, Davis." The way she says my name, flashbacks of our night in Deacon fill my mind.

"Night, T. Get some sleep."

One week later

TEAGAN and I have fallen into a bit of a routine. We start our mornings with a short text exchange, and at night, we talk until she sounds sleepy, and we have to go to bed to start the day over again. Throughout the day, I find myself thinking of her, and I can't wait until I get to talk to her again. So far, we've kept things light. Occasionally, we'll get into something deeper, but we mostly just talk about our days, how Connor is doing, and some of the things four year olds get themselves into.

Apparently, his cast isn't slowing him down. He's dying to ride his bike—which his mom thankfully refuses. He had just learned to ride without training wheels, and it wouldn't be in his best interest to do activities like that yet.

I've quickly learned she's only a morning person out of necessity. Like me, coffee is her friend. She uses it to help her through the day, because her alarm goes off at five, so she can get Connor to daycare and herself to work on time. She mostly works from home, but occasionally has to go into the office. She sets her hours early, so she can spend more time with Connor while he's awake in the evenings. I still don't know what's up with Connor's dad, but since she's never mentioned him, I don't get the idea he's been in the picture. I'm sure it'll come up in time, but until she's ready, I'll let her take the lead.

As if she knows I'm thinking of her on my lunch break, a text vibrates my phone.

As soon as I swipe open my screen, I expect a simple text. Instead, there's an image. When I click on it, my entire screen fills with a picture of a multi-colored rooster and her beautiful face. The caption reads:

Teagan: Saw this at a home goods store and thought of you.

Me: It's beautiful—and I'm not talking about the giant cock.

Teagan: Maybe I should get it for you as a housewarming gift when you find a place of your own.

Me: Or not.

Me: Unless you mean I get you as a housewarming gift. I may be up for that suggestion.

Rereading that text, my heart stalls.
Fuck—she could read it as I want her to move in instead of the chicken.

Teagan: You'll be up all night. If I'm not mistaken, it has magical powers and knows how to wring out Os.

If I thought I couldn't breathe before, nothing prepares me for that message. Unfortunately, I've just taken a drink of water and literally spit it everywhere across the table, making everyone in the entire cafeteria look at me.

"Whoops, wrong pipe," I announce to the room when I frantically clean up the table around me. A nice lady brings me another napkin, and I'm not sure what's redder, my ears or the cherry tomatoes in my salad.

Teagan: Hello? Are you there?

Teagan: Where did you go?

When I get control of myself, I quickly reply.

Me: You really should give a guy some warning before talking about magical cocks. I am in no way complaining—but I was NOT PREPARED!!!

Me: If you're worried I'll have an inflated ego—you should know—I just humiliated myself in the cafeteria by spewing my drink everywhere.

Me: I'll never be able to eat in here again, and I just started working here, so that sucks.

Me: Though now all I can think about is using my magical cock.

Teagan: LMAO—Sorry—Not sorry. (winky face emoji)

Me: How many weeks again?

Teagan: Too many.

Me: I gotta run. Have to meet a patient. Have fun with your cock.

Me: Wish it were me.

Chapter 12

Teagan

Two weeks left...

IT'S BEEN A LONG DAY. Connor wakes up at the ass crack of dawn and is bright eyed and bushy tailed, ready to start his day. I try to get him to come lie down with me, just so I can sleep that last hour before my alarm, but he isn't having it. Even though he naps at daycare, I can tell he's a little wired. With it only being four in the afternoon, I know I have to keep him up until at least seven, or the vicious cycle will continue.

Normally, I'd take him to the park to wear off his extra energy, but since he can't play on any of the toys today, that'd just be mean. "What do you want to do tonight, sweet boy?" I ask through my rearview mirror on our way home from daycare.

"Pizza and a show."

That won't tire him out, so I suggest, "Wanna go for a walk first?"

He nods from the back seat as I pull into our driveway.

After we take our things inside, I order our pizza and see we have plenty of time to go for a walk before it arrives. Just as we get out of the driveway, he asks, "When is Aunt Annie comin'? I miss her."

"She's working on a big project at work tonight, but we can invite her over this weekend to watch the Renegades play. How does that sound?"

"Yay! Can you make dip?" He's referring to my seven-layer dip he loves.

"I think I can handle that. How's your arm today?"

"It's fine, but itchy. How many more sleeps until I get it off?"

He still has a hard time understanding days of the week, let alone days in a month, so I set up a calendar for him and each day when he wakes up, we put a sticker on the calendar to show how much closer we are to his next appointment. I have no idea who's more excited, him or me, about him getting his cast off. Not only would it mean he can shower again, but it also means I'll see Davis in person.

"Just thirteen more days. It'll be over before we know it. Are you hurting at all?"

He shrugs as his head shakes, "No. Just itchy."

"Remember what Dr. Fallon said. Whatever you do, please don't stick anything down your cast to scratch it. It could get lost and hurt you more." The other night, he told me about a pen getting stuck in a boy's cast and caused more damage than necessary. Not to mention, it was gross when it got pulled out. Yuck.

Sighing heavily, he says, "I won't, but my hand's itchy."

"Just let me know if it bugs you too much, m'kay?"

The moment the mail truck stops in front of our house,

Connor runs to the window and announces, "There's a package!"

Not expecting anything, I wonder if my mom has sent something.

He has to wait for me to undo the top lock of our front door, but the moment I release it, the door bursts open, and he runs to the front porch to see what it is.

We live in an older kid-friendly neighborhood. Many of our neighbors have kids, and Connor knows not to go past the edge of our yard when he's outside, so I don't worry about him going ahead of me. There's a wide sidewalk and a patch of grass between that and the curb of the street, so it leaves plenty of leeway for Connor to play safely in the front yard, if I have to run into the house for anything. Cars typically drive slow enough, but I'm not willing to risk that chance, therefore I'm strict with our rule.

As I enter the porch, I hear his excitement wain slightly. "It's for you." My mom sends him enough packages now that he's learned how to read and write his own name. She likes to send him letters and small presents through the mail, and he draws her a picture in exchange. He loves getting the mail each day because we never know when she'll surprise him.

Seeing as it's not from my mom, I rack my brain wondering if I've forgotten an order or something, but I keep coming up blank. Taking it inside, I head to the kitchen to open the tape with scissors.

My jaw drops to the floor when I find a brand-new e-reader inside.

One I clearly didn't order. I had mentioned the other night

I needed a new one because mine is out of storage and doesn't keep a charge. I'd been irritated because my favorite romantic suspense author, Brittney Sahin, had just dropped another book, and I couldn't read it on release day because I had to charge my device.

This feels too good to be true.

"What is it, Mommy?"

Holding it up in disbelief, I just stare at this thoughtful gift. This has been on my list of things to buy, but I just haven't gotten around to it yet. "I... uh... got a new e-reader."

As I stare at the new top-notch device, my chest tightens. It's been years since someone besides my mom has done anything this thoughtful—let alone surprise me.

When Connor laughs, my attention is suddenly on him. "What's so funny?"

Pointing to the box, he giggles some more. "That is."

How the hell had I missed that?

If I wasn't certain who the gift was from before, there's no doubt now. There, right under the packaging Connor had removed, is a cover for the kindle—with a giant rooster face staring back at me. He'd obviously custom picked the design because the image is the exact replica of the one we stood in front of just a few weeks ago.

"Buk, Buk, Buuuuk," Connor innocently clucks, and I lose all sense of myself, right then and there.

I laugh so hard tears stream down my face, and I have to hold on to the counter while crossing my legs, so I don't wet myself from my sudden coughing fit. Gasping for air, I can only laugh harder when Connor clucks like a chicken again.

He did not just do that.

Oh, but he has—and holy hell, I think I might die.

And the stinker does it again because he loves my reaction —which only makes me laugh harder. Gasping for air, I do my best to stand upright, while keeping my legs crossed.

When I finally get my wits about me, I grab my phone and record Connor clucking like a chicken and doing a chicken walk with his cast and good arm, all while stretching his neck to his new rhythmic beat. As soon as I get enough to prove my point, I flip my camera to me and add through fits of laughter, "Oh my God... best gift... ever." Taking a deep breath to control my speaking, I shake my head. "But I entirely blame you for creating this." Then point the video back to Connor before cutting it off and pressing send before I can think better of it.

I'm sure Davis is working for another hour or so, and I don't expect to hear from him. So, after calming down, I take care of some things in the kitchen, while Connor takes off down the hall to his bedroom for something.

I'm surprised when a text notification arrives.

Davis: Mission accomplished! Glad you liked it.

Another chime.

Davis: His reaction is priceless. I can't wait to hear about it in further detail tonight when we talk.

Me: Oh, it was. We're going for a walk in a bit before dinner.

Davis: I love texting and phone calls, but do you think we could video chat tonight? I've really missed that gorgeous face of yours.

Me: You're not so bad yourself. It's a date.

Me: Not a date—for a few more weeks—but you know what I mean. (winky emoji)

Davis: I'm looking forward to tonight. I'll be home around seven, so call once Connor is down for the count.

Me: Will do.

With a little bounce in my step, I head to Connor's room. If we're getting a walk in, we'd better do it sooner than later.

INSTEAD OF TEXTING OR CALLING, like I usually do, I eagerly press the button for video. While I wait for him to answer, my belly flips in anticipation. Even though I've talked to him nearly every day over the past few weeks, it's been way too long since I've seen his facial expressions live. His pictures from Texas don't hold a candle to the real thing, and I'd be lying if I said I didn't miss him.

Just when I think he might not answer, his devastatingly handsome face fills my screen. "Hey, you! Sorry it took me so long. I'd left my phone in the other room."

"How was your day?" I ask with interest.

He fills me in on his one surgery this morning, then explains how he saw other patients for consults or follow-ups. Overall, it was a productive day. I can't imagine having such an impactful job. It nearly killed me watching Connor hurt and knowing there was nothing I could do for him, but Davis gets to rush in and save the day on a regular basis—like a superhero.

Of course, he'd never see it like that. He's humble when it comes to downplaying the fact that this thirteen-year-old he helped today will have a chance to compete in competitive gymnastics again, thanks to him. Anyone in Davis's position could have an ego the size of Alaska—or a god complex, but the more I get to know him, the more I realize just how genuine and thoughtful he is. He cares about his patients and wants what's best for them.

Eventually, he asks how the clucking video came to be, and I give him the play-by-play. He and I both are in fits of laughter by the end. Once he's calmed down, he admits, "I couldn't help it. Once I saw the custom covers as an option, I just had to get it for you."

"You didn't have to do anything, Davis. You know that, right?" I'm very privileged as a single mom who happens to be a software engineer. I have a great job and don't need any assistance from anyone. It's a sense of accomplishment I've worked hard to live up to over the years.

"I know, but you were on my mind when I one-clicked… and well, the rest is history. Besides, now that we know Connor loves chickens, too, how can it not be our thing?"

Our thing.

The way he says it gives me hope of a future with him.

For all I know, we could get past this moratorium on dating and when I'm no longer forbidden fruit—so to say—I won't be as tempting.

"Where did you go?" he asks, pulling me out of my revelry.

"Just thinking you might be too good to be true," I admit on a sigh.

Rolling his eyes, he humbly admits, "I don't know about that, but I'm here, and I'm real."

"You're sure it's not just that there's some magic in the mystery? I mean, I'm sure I'll scare you off once we get to know each other better."

"Mmmm…" Even I can tell he's only pretending to think. "I highly doubt it. The more I see, the more I like."

"Hopefully, you'll feel the same when I bring a cranky four-year-old in need of a nap around."

"I hear what you're saying, but I'm fairly certain that unless he truly hates me, anything he does won't be much of a problem. I'm used to cranky kids all the time. I get them tired, scared, and in pain. He can't be much worse than that."

"I doubt he could hate you," I admit, but keep my next thought to myself.

If he likes you just one-tenth of how much I do, then we shouldn't have any problems there.

Holy shit—where did that come from?

"Speaking of Connor..." Davis's tone shifts as if something is causing him to hesitate.

"Yes..." I draw out to prompt him further. Whatever he needs to say, he should so we can clear the air and deal with it.

"It's just that you've never mentioned his father, and I've gotten the impression he's no longer in the picture."

I've answered this question a million times, but with Davis, I feel I need to go beyond my normal glazed-over answer. "Um..." Where to begin. I may as well start with the beginning... "Jacob never met Connor as he died in a car accident before Connor was born."

Chapter 13

Davis

HOLY SHIT. *I did not see that coming.*

It takes me a moment to process what she's said, and my heart goes out to both her and Connor for never knowing his father. I can't imagine what it's been like raising Connor alone. Well, I know she has a support system, but it's not the same as having a partner. "I'm so sorry for your loss."

Teagan takes in a low and steady breath. "Thank you."

For a while, neither of us say anything, and I'm completely floundering for what to say next after the bomb she just dropped.

But before I'm forced to flop on dry land for too long, she quietly adds, "Not many people know beyond what I've told you, but to be honest, my feelings for Jacob have been all over the place since his death.

"You see, we'd been fighting that day, so for years, I've felt tremendous guilt, then anger over the entire situation. But knowing I can't hold onto those feelings for Connor's sake, I've worked through my feelings and tried my best to let them go."

"What do you mean?" I ask for clarification because this is certainly not the time to make assumptions.

Sighing heavily, I see her glance up at the ceiling before returning to the screen. The anguish on her expression makes me want to reach through the phone and hold her. It kills me to be this far away if we're having a conversation like this. But then again, maybe she'll feel less vulnerable with this distance. Either way, if she wants to share, I will support her in any way she'll let me.

When she remains quiet, I quickly give her an out. "You don't have to tell me. I'm not trying to pry."

"No, it's probably best that you know. I've just only told a few people about the actual events surrounding his death because I never wanted anyone to judge him. But you also need to know my truth."

Holy shit. What the hell happened?

Leaning back onto her pillow, I see her settle herself and adjust the pillow until she's comfortable. "You see, Jacob and I were college sweethearts. We met at the end of our junior year. He was pre-law and as you know, I was a computer science major. We hit it off and before we knew it, we had a five-year plan for how we'd proceed. He was to go to law school right after undergrad. Since I can work from basically anywhere, we agreed I'd follow him to any law school he got accepted. Then after he graduated, we'd get married."

She's quiet for a moment, and I can sense there's more to the story, so I prompt, "But..."

"But with one semester left of our senior year, we found out I was pregnant, and he panicked. Well, freaked out is a better term. Instead of being excited about our future, all he saw was the monstrous amount of debt he'd accrue for the next few years and his inability to provide for me and a child.

"He told me he needed some space to think about things. This is how he always reacted to big changes. He'd go away and process, then come back, and we'd deal with them head-on. Apparently, he ended up at a bar with one of his buddies—where he proceeded to get shit-faced drunk. He wasn't a big drinker, so the fact that he went to a bar makes me realize he *was* freaking out and not actually processing."

She runs a hand down her face as she sighs heavily. "Eventually, I'd called him to find out where he was. Normally, he'd just go for a run or something, but it'd been almost an entire day since I'd heard from him, and I'd begun to worry.

"When I realized I'd been worrying about him for the better part of a day—all while he'd been getting drunk off his ass—well, I got pissed. I said a few things to him in the heat of the moment, and among them was *this baby and I would be better off without him if this is how he was going to handle things.* I'd hung up the phone and was so hormonal, I turned off my phone entirely. I didn't want to hear from him if this is what he considered handling it.

"Since it was still early in the evening, I eventually turned on my phone to use it for something else. That's when I saw he'd called. At first, I was so angry with him, I didn't even want to listen to the message, but eventually, curiosity got the better of me, so I did."

So far, Teagan's voice has been steady, as if she's just reciting the facts, but when her voice cracks, so does my heart.

"He... he... told me he'd made a mistake. That he loved me so much and that he couldn't handle me being mad at him. He said he was so sorry, and he wanted to raise our baby together. He told me he loved me and our unborn baby. He was just scared. He didn't know how it would work out, but he was determined we'd find a way."

God, please tell me he didn't drive home.

I barely make out the words when she whispers after a long moment of silence. "But he never came home."

A tear rolling down her cheek is my undoing. Through watery eyes of my own, I see her steady her breath and continue her horrific story.

"I waited." She gasps out. Then she takes another breath as tears pour down her cheeks. I'd fucking give anything to prevent her from hurting any further. Each breath she takes to steady herself guts me open further.

Her voice is so quiet when she eventually explains, "I waited for hours for him to arrive. Eventually, there was a knock at the door, so I rushed to answer it."

She takes a tissue and wipes at her eyes before continuing, "But instead of Jacob standing on the other side, it was his roommate. The moment I saw his red-rimmed eyes, I knew. I just knew with every fiber of my being that something bad had happened." She's sobbing by this point and after she sucks in another breath, she's quiet for a long moment.

"You don't have to tell me anymore," I croak out, drowning in emotion. "I can't put you through any more pain."

Shaking her head, this beautiful, strong woman says, "No. It's best you know. Jacob had gone to the bar with his roommates to get drunk because he was freaking out about the baby. But after I gave him the what-for, he apparently pulled his head out of his ass and decided he wanted to be the best father possible to our unborn child. He was bound and determined to get to me so he could tell me in person—since I hadn't picked up my phone."

Shit. I know where this is going. "Did he..." I start, but she cuts me off.

"He didn't drive home if that's what you're thinking. No—he took an Uber. They were about six blocks from my apartment when a truck ran a light and T-boned the car Jacob was riding in. Apparently, he died on impact and probably didn't see it coming—or at least that's what the driver who survived told the police before being airlifted for spinal injuries.

"I'd heard some sirens but didn't think anything about it, as we lived near a fire station. The truck slammed directly into Jacob's door. I can only hope he didn't suffer."

Holy shit. That's fucking tragic.

"I'm so sorry, Teagan." My words aren't nearly enough. It takes everything in me not to drive to her house and just hold her. She only lives ten minutes away. I could hop in my car and go—but she needs to finish this story—so I remain planted on my bed.

"Only my best friend, Annie, knows the entire story I've just shared. I couldn't let his parents or mine know we'd had a fight, and I was partially to blame for his death. Of course, I know differently—now. I had nothing to do with it, and I've come to terms with the accident. But at the time, I just couldn't tarnish his memory—and now, it wouldn't have changed the outcome."

She laughs once without humor, then quickly adds, "You met his parents at the hospital. They've tried to be involved in Connor's life as much as possible. I bring him to Texas once a year, and they travel here when they can to visit. We also try to video chat regularly.

"Dianne and Jim are two of the kindest people I've ever known. They knew Jacob loved me, and I just couldn't tell them we'd had a fight because Jacob had a weak moment and freaked out. Many new parents do the same. He shouldn't be remembered for that one instance. Besides, I'd never want Connor to know there was even a moment his dad didn't want him."

Holy shit. How do I even process everything? This was so not where I thought things would go tonight. I feel honored she trusts me enough to tell me the entire story. It puts a lot of things into perspective.

"Thank you for sharing this, Teagan. I'm sure things haven't been easy for you, but you are one of the most kind and selfless people I know. I'd give anything to just hug you right now."

"Same," she admits. "It's taken me years of therapy and a lot of hard work to get to where I am today. I have peace knowing Jacob loved me—I never doubted that. I also know he loved Connor without a doubt. He had a huge heart but a weak moment."

And this—right here, might just be the moment I completely fall in love with Teagan Frost.

Chapter 14
Davis

IT'S BEEN a little over a week since Teagan revealed her truth of how she became a single mom and each day since, we grow closer to one another. With only a few days left until we see each other in person, I hope like hell this connection I feel between us is real and not just a pipe dream we've built in this bubble we've stayed in.

I keep waiting for the bubble to burst, but with each new hidden facet I find about her, the more I'm intrigued. I'll admit I'm nervous to see if this is real. For now, I guess I just have to be content with texting each morning and video chatting each evening after Connor's fast asleep.

So that I don't royally fuck it up, I've spent hours researching how to date a single mom. As a doctor, I deal in numbers and statistics, clinical trials and case studies. Even after reading multiple articles, I'm happy to find my thoughts or beliefs on the matter haven't changed—as I've always thought Connor should come first. Juggling our chaotic schedules could become problematic, but so far, nothing seems out of reach. Patience is key and giving one another grace. But

I also know theory and reality are sometimes two different entities.

I could research this until the cows come home, but nothing gives me a concrete path to follow. As self-doubt creeps in, I do what I should've done in the first place. Call my brother Damien.

"Whoa… Davy's calling me, and I didn't even text first. To what do I owe the honor?"

Yeah, I'm known to never initiate calls. Usually, I'll text a quick message if I need something answered. I haven't had a lot of time for chitchat with med school, but everyone knows I'd be there for them in a heartbeat if they ever need anything. They also enjoy being complete asshats and tease me when they can—it's what we do. A Fallon family tradition, so to say.

I ignore his comment and cut to the chase. "When you met Vanessa, how did you navigate the situation with Jules?"

Vanessa and Damien have been married for about five years. She was a single mom when they met. Julia—or Jules as we call her—had just turned five. Hopefully, he'll have some sound advice to share with me.

"Well, hello to you, too." I can hear the smile in his voice as he walks away from the noise on his end of the line. "Give me a sec. I think I need to sit down for this."

"Sorry if I called at a bad time." Hell, he has three kids under ten. There's never a quiet time at his house, especially in the evenings.

But is that a bad thing? He has chaos, laughter, and so much love. As much as I love my single life, I'll admit seeing each of my siblings fall for their perfect match is kind of awesome all the same.

Maybe someday that will happen to me, too.

"Nah. They'll survive for a while. Syd and Vince brought Everett and Emery to play with the boys. But Jules and Van have them occupied for the time being. Besides, now I need to know why you'd call and ask such a question."

Yeah, this is out of the ordinary—even for me. I rarely come to him for advice—especially about women. Mainly because I've never stuck around long enough to warrant needing relationship advice with someone because it hardly lasts beyond the bedroom.

"I met a girl..." I start but stop because I don't know where to start, or how much to reveal.

"Okay, captain obvious. I figured that much out."

Fuck it. This is Dame; he won't judge me.

"I actually met Teagan at the B&B in Deacon."

"Wait, you're not moving, are you?"

"Hell no. I just landed my dream job, and I'm finally back in Washington."

"Good... Then explain because I'm confused. Who is Teagan, and why are you suddenly interested in how I handled things with Van and Jules?"

I quickly explain that how, on the day I'd met her, I thought it would be just like any other girl I hook up with on occasion. Of course, I keep some details to myself, but he gets the CliffNotes version of how we met. Right up until I came back from coffee and she was gone.

"Holy shit, that must have been a shock. The roles being reversed and all."

"Not gonna lie. I was bummed. I thought I'd read the situation all wrong and couldn't for the life of me figure out where she'd gone. But then I got called into the hospital and had to put her out of my mind. There was a four-year-old who had chipped the end of his elbow off, and he needed my attention more than my ego."

"Ouch—on both accounts."

"You'll never guess who was in the room when I walked in to see my new patient... Teagan, that's who. Not only was I shocked as hell to see her there, but I had to pretend like I didn't just spend the entire evening getting to know every inch of her. Of course, I gave her the option of calling in another surgeon, but since I had more experience with this type of surgery, it made sense that I stay on the case. Besides—I could also follow-up as I was moving to Seattle."

"Wait, she lives here?"

"Catch up, Dame. Of course, she lives here. There's no way I'd do a long-term relationship with distance. It just wouldn't work. I'll be lucky if I don't fuck this up as it is."

"I'm sure you'll figure it out, Davy. Don't be so hard on yourself. Not to be a bearer of bad news, but isn't there an issue with you being involved with a patient's parent?"

Sighing heavily, "Yes... and I won't do anything with her again until he's no longer my patient."

"That's probably a good idea. But do you even know if she's interested in more?"

"Yeah. I do...." I draw out, knowing I need to tell him

everything if I want his help. "Technically, I've only seen her in person at his one appointment here in Seattle. But ever since that first appointment four weeks ago, we've talked nearly every day. I know—I'm coloring outside the lines with this one—or at least heavily in the gray area, but there's something about her I just can't walk away from."

"This is huge, Davy. I don't think I've ever heard you talk about anyone like this."

"And that's exactly why I don't want to fuck it up. Every aspect of this situation with Teagan is uncharted territory for me. I don't do strings—let alone knowingly try for more when there's a kid involved. But with her, the strings don't even come close to bothering me."

"That's how you know, man." I swear I can hear his shrug as if that explains everything.

Which of course it doesn't.

"What the hell is that supposed to mean? Explain."

"You know as well as I do that I wasn't looking for Vanessa or Jules. I'd just started a new job and had no intentions of staying near Columbia River University for more than one year. All I did was go to a diner off campus and found myself coming back day after day—and it wasn't for the food or the grumpy old man next to me—though he's still one of my best friends. We all know damn well the reason I went back is Vanessa. I can't explain it—but I just knew she was the one."

"But how did Jules handle you coming around?"

Damien laughs once hard. "Ha... Jules... well, she gave me the what-for. She in no uncertain terms asked my intentions. Then that day she told me she loved me, I knew I'd fallen just as hard for her. Hell, I still get teary when I remember how upset she was when she found out Van wasn't my fiancée—and she was convinced I didn't want them. There's nothing like getting your ass handed to you by a five-year-old. They are way more perceptive than they let on."

"Yeah." I remember the story, but he's not getting my point. "*How* did you navigate getting to know Jules? I'm around kids every day, but I've never tried dating their mom."

"Oh," as if he's just clued in to what I'm asking. "I took my lead from Vanessa. But, Davy—you're not just dating his mom. You're essentially dating him, too—that sounds weird, but you know what I mean. No matter how much Vanessa loved me, I knew Jules always came first, and I never considered putting Van in a situation where she'd have to choose."

"Okay..." That sounds simple enough. Then another thought hits me. "But how do I go from being his doctor to the one dating his mom?"

"Van might be able to give you more insight on that, but single moms are special. If they're letting you in—it means you already mean something to them. They don't have time for games or people who don't have their shit together. If you're into Teagan—be all in. Anything less isn't fair to her or her son. If it doesn't work out, it won't. There are no guarantees in life —but if you think she's worth the risk, I'm sure you'll relish the reward."

"Whoa... slow your roll, brother. You sound like I'm gonna be married like you, in months."

I can hear the smile through the phone. "Best decision of my life—well, of Jules' life—we all know how that went down.

But seriously consider this... Don't jump the gun, but if you decide she's the one, what's the point of waiting?"

I'm still in awe of how he just knew—same with Derek. I've always thought they were crazy, but now I'm not so sure.

"Davy," Damien warns. "I can hear your wheels spinning. Relax. Nothing has to be decided today."

"Dad... do you know where the UNO cards are?" I hear yelling through the phone.

"I'll help you find them when I get off the phone with Uncle Davy."

"Really, lemme talk to him."

Dame doesn't even ask as he hands over his phone to his oldest. He knows if I'm free, I'll always talk to Jules. "Hey, Uncle Davy. When will we see you again?"

"I'll be at the next Renegades home game. Will you be there?" I'm certain Dani said everyone is coming to that game as it's a big one against Denver. I think Derek and Tessa will even come back to town for it.

"Dad, are we going to the next game?" Dame must nod his answer because I suddenly hear Jules gush, "Yeah. We'll be there. I've missed you so much! I want another movie night with you. Can we have a slumber party at your house?"

"Uh... I'm still staying at Derek and Tessa's. I'm not sure Melody will approve of that."

"Still... it's been forever since I spent the night with you. Maybe you can come here soon, and my brothers can go to Unks' house for the night." Unks is her nickname for Vince, Vanessa's twin brother.

"That hardly seems fair to your brothers," I point out but

secretly, I'm dying with laughter inside. She's never been afraid to speak her mind. When she met Dame, she didn't just get one guy to fall for her—my entire family did.

"Still. You were gone so long. I miss you."

"I've missed you, too, Jules. I promise we'll spend time together soon."

"Okay... here's Dad. I need to go find those cards for the boys."

When Damien gets back on the phone, I ask the question that struck while talking with Jules. "Do you think it would be weird to get tickets for Teagan and Connor to come to the game? They're huge fans, and it would make his day to possibly meet some of the players. But our family is huge, and it could be overwhelming."

"Only you can answer that. You know how we are—the more the merrier, but we could also scare the pants right off her and send her running in the other direction with our brood. But—Mom and Dad are still traveling in Greece this week, so we do have two extra tickets. Just food for thought."

"Hmmm.... I'll have to think about it."

Chapter 15

Teagan

One more day...

I'VE JUST TUCKED Connor into bed, and I'm tinkering in the kitchen, cleaning up from dinner when a text comes through.

Swiping open my phone, I'm confused when I see a picture of the Renegades stadium. But my mouth drops when I read the caption to the text.

Davis: Can I take you and Connor to the game next weekend?

Immediately, I press the call button instead of responding. This is too important to text about. The moment he answers, I say, "Are you freaking kidding me?"

"Well, hi to you, too! How was your day?"

"Really? That's what you're opening with?" It's like he doesn't comprehend my level of excitement.

Amused, he asks, "What?"

"You just invited Connor and me to a Rainier Renegades game, like it isn't a big deal. You know we're huge fans."

"Uh… to be honest, it isn't that big of a deal."

What? Why does he sound apprehensive? He should be excited for this. I know I am. His voice seems off, so I quickly suggest, "Can we video chat?"

I don't even give him a chance before I hang up and press the video option.

Once again, he's laughing when the call picks up. He's clean shaven and still wearing his shirt and tie from work. "What's going on, T? Talk to me."

"Why don't you think it's a big deal?"

Cringing, he says, "I've told you about Luke, right? You know—Dani's husband."

"Yeah, you've mentioned they live between Anderson Island and Tacoma, and they have two kids, why?"

"I, uh… shit. I guess I've never mentioned why my family and I often go to the games, have I?"

"I know you're huge fans and have season tickets, but what does that have to do with Luke?"

"My sister's married to Luke Leighton, the Renegades head coach. I… uh… guess I forgot that part."

"What the actual frickity frack are you talking about? How could you not tell me?" Thinking back through our conversations, even from our very first day, he's always just said he was a big fan of Rainier. But wait… that first day… he had used the words, *he had to be*… Now, it makes sense.

"It never came up. I just kinda forgot you didn't know."

"Any other famous people in your family you've forgotten to mention?"

Davis runs a hand down his face and cringes again. "That depends."

"On?"

"Do you follow the romance industry? My sister—who will always be just Dani to me—because that's weird, writes under the pen name Charlotte Ann."

I'd have to be living under a rock not to know her name, but instead of being snarky, I just nod. "I've heard of her. Any more celebrities you want to pull out of your ass while we're at it? Got a famous uncle or grandparent I don't know about?" I tease instead.

He looks sheepishly with a shrug into the phone. "Nope, that's about it."

Smiling, he shakes his head. "God, you're adorable when you're caught off guard, you know that? Well, I think you're sexy when you get excited. Now that I know you like surprises, I'll have to do them more often."

Who doesn't like surprises? Instead, I'm caught off guard by Davis loosening his tie and unbuttoning his top few buttons. When he stops, I'm almost begging for more to be revealed. Memories of our first night together flash through my mind as heat spreads throughout my body.

"What's going on in that head of yours, T?"

Instantly, my cheeks heat at being caught ogling. "Just enjoying the view," I quietly admit.

"Well..." His voice is suddenly much deeper. "Why don't you go into your bedroom and you can tell me exactly what you're thinking because if I had to bet, I'd say it was a lot more than that. Your cheeks are a magnificent shade of pink in this moment."

I don't even hesitate. I walk the few steps to my bedroom, which is located on the other side of my kitchen. Connor's room is at the other end of my house, and Davis knows I like to be in my bedroom so I don't wake him.

The moment the door clicks shut, Davis's sexy voice practically purrs. "Tell me what you were thinking out there."

My throat suddenly dries as I admit on a whisper, "I was remembering our first night together and um..."

As he slips his tie off, my core clenches and heart races. "Hmmm... and just what were you thinking about? Words—use them, Teagan. You know I like to hear them."

We've been flirty on the phone for the last week or so, and even on the edge of taking it further, but we've always kept it innocent enough. But the heat in his eyes, and the tone of his voice, makes me want to push things further. After tomorrow—we'll hopefully be able to see one another again—and I'd be a flat-out liar if I didn't admit I'm dying for a replay of that night. Hell, I've practically worn out my vibrator thinking about it—after Davis and I get off the phone a few times. Thank God for rechargeable batteries.

"God, you were so sexy when you blindfolded me. But right now, I'm wishing I could see you without your shirt on again."

"Really?" he asks as he undoes another button. "I'm pretty sure I can do that for you."

I watch as he sets the phone down and positions it so I can

see more of him, standing next to his bed. "You mean like this?" he asks as he slowly does the most magnificent silent strip tease. "You lick that lip again, and next time we're alone together, I get to do it for you, Teagan."

"Is that so?" I ask, feigning innocence, then lick my lower lip deliberately.

"I've been trying to be good these past eight weeks, but right now, I want to get in my car, drive to your house, and lick every square inch of your body. I deserve an award for the type of restraint I've displayed these past two months."

"You and me both," I tease. "You're standing there all sexy, running your fingers through your hair. It turns me on, Davis. Hell, I've been fantasizing about our night together since I've been home. It's a good thing my vibrator has a wall charger, or I'd go broke if I had to buy batteries."

"You are so fucking sexy, Teagan. I'd give anything to watch you do that."

Feeling much braver than I am, I boldly throw down a challenge. "Only if I get to watch your face as you come with me?"

For a moment, he's frozen in place. At first, I think maybe we have a bad connection, but then his voice cracks as he warns, "Don't make promises you don't intend to keep."

Heat floods my body as my need for this man grows stronger. "Tell me what you're thinking," I prompt. I love his bossy side and hope in this moment more than anything, I get to see it.

"Oh, Teagan." The words sound so sexy coming from his lips. "I'm not sure you want to know all the thoughts racing through my brain." Reaching down, I see his hand disappear under the screen, just below his belly button, and I can only imagine he's adjusting himself.

God, I wish it were my hand doing that. "I'm pretty sure by the expression on your face that I do."

His voice is sexy as hell when he demands, "Get your vibrator and get yourself comfortable on that bed. I don't have to see anything but your face, but I need to watch you come—is what's on my mind. You sure you want to hear that?"

Walking to my dresser, I find myself doing just that. Electricity zings through my body and just pulling out my favorite personal friend has me dripping with need. "I want to hear everything that's on your mind. Since you can't be here to touch me physically, I need to hear every word."

"Get on the bed and get yourself comfortable. Adjust the phone so it focuses on your beautiful face. You are exquisite to watch when you come apart, and I've missed you so much."

Feeling brave as I walk to my bed, I rip my shirt over my head and reveal that I've already ditched my bra for the night. He can't see my full breasts in the screen, but my cleavage is on full display for him.

I hear him take in a breath and see him close his eyes momentarily.

"Everything okay?" I ask for reassurance he still wants this.

Even through the phone when his lids open, his eyes are liquid heat when they pierce into me. "Teagan, you are the most beautiful woman on this planet. I love the way your breath catches when you get turned on. I also love how soft your skin is as well as how wet you get when I've barely touched you. The next time we're alone, I have so many things I want to do with you."

"Tell me," I encourage and watch his arm move down again. "First, I want to kiss and caress each breast until they are tender and driving you wild with need. I'll lick, squeeze, and pull your nipples until you make that sound at the back of your throat, which makes me harder than granite. In the meantime, take off your pants and slide your fingers into your panties."

He waits until I do just that, then with a sexy as hell tone, that's as smooth as butter and excites the hell out of me, he says, "Are you doing that?"

"Yes," I sigh, just as my finger finds my clit. With the phone propped up on a pillow near me, I have two hands free, and I look into the phone to see his arms moving in a motion that shows he's clearly touching himself. "Tell me what you're doing to yourself."

"Sliding my hand up and down my cock. With your free hand, squeeze one of our breasts to make your nipples harden. I know how much you like it when I suck them in my mouth. Sorry I can't be there to do it myself, but I want you to get your vibrator and turn it on."

After pressing the button, it zings to life and a low, quiet buzz fills the room.

"Before you use it where you need it most, I want you to bring it up and over each of your nipples slowly."

Having never done that before, I'm surprised when the vibration takes over every nerve ending and zips down my spine, making my inner muscles contract. "Oh, God, that feels good," I moan.

"Keep doing that to your beautiful breasts while you circle your clit with your other hand. Imagine me teasing you, dipping inside you, and bringing my fingers along your slit to circle your clit again."

Between his words, the vibrator, and my fingers, I'm soaring higher and higher, faster than I could have imagined. "Now, slowly drag the vibrator over your ribs and down to where you need it most. I'm not sure what you like, so I want you to find your sure-fire way to make you come hardest."

He smiles triumphantly the moment he knows I have it just where I need it. "Someday soon, I'm going to do that to you. You're going to show me how you like it, and I'll be the one controlling the vibrator, while kissing you everywhere. In fact, I'm dying to use a vibrator on you while I'm eating you out. I fucking love the way you taste... God, Teagan, this is so hot... you are so fucking beautiful."

His moan causes ripples of energy to flow through me, and the base of my spine tightens. My nerve endings coil in, and I can't help but let my head fall back and relish each wave of heat that explodes through my body. From the roots of my hair to the tips of my toes, I feel the ripples of ecstasy flow through me.

Pulse after pulse, waves of energy flow up and down my spine, spreading from the tips of my toes and over every square inch of my body. Right as I'm hitting my peak, his voice roars through the phone, "You are so fucking beautiful, Teagan. Not only are you sexy as fuck but responsive."

Clicking off the vibrator, my room is suddenly silent. Shyly, I smile into the phone. "Hey, you."

"Hey, yourself, T. Next time we're alone, I want to watch the rest of you do that."

Sighing heavily in my state of bliss, I say, "I think that can be arranged. Sorry, I couldn't think enough to reciprocate. This is a first for me, and I feel like I left you hanging."

The sexiest grin spreads across his face, and my stomach flips. "Oh, you didn't leave me behind. I never in a million years thought when I woke up this morning, this is how my night will end, but you will *never* hear me complain if I'm spending time with you."

I want to touch him and feel his body against mine. It's been far too long.

"Do you think Connor will be cleared tomorrow? I'm not sure I can wait much longer to see you."

"We'll have to see the x-rays, but from the way he was progressing, it's a strong possibility. If he does, can I see you tomorrow night?"

And just like that, my libido springs back to life, and I boldly lay down another challenge. "Only if you wear that tie we used in Texas."

Chapter 16
Davis

IT'S BEEN A LONG DAY. Not only did I stay up chatting with Teagan long after we made each other come twice over the phone, but I had an early surgery this morning to repair a ten year old's clavicle. He'd broken it when the vehicle he'd been riding in rolled before landing in a ditch. Thankfully, that was the worst of the injuries, but added to the afternoon of patients I have scheduled, I'm ready for my last appointment of the day—Connor Frost.

Even though the day dragged on, I'm eager to see Teagan and find myself wired in anticipation. I seriously hope like hell Connor's arm has healed—not only for his sake—but for the fact that I'm dying to officially be able to see Teagan in public. I'm not sure I can take being apart from her much longer.

Unfortunately, by the time they are set to arrive, I'm running behind schedule. To help save them from waiting too long, I've asked Miss Carol to meet them and take Connor to remove the cast and have images taken.

Between patients, I personally reach out to Teagan to let her know the plan. There's no way in hell I want her thinking I'm blowing her off. Hopefully, I'll be done with this last consult for a potential torn meniscus soon, so I can move on to Connor and Teagan.

When I finally knock on the door to the exam room, my heart races like a teenager picking up their first date. I swear my palms get sweaty. This hasn't happened to me since I entered the room for the first time flying solo in med school. Not only am I nervous to see Teagan in person, but I'm eager to find the prognosis of Connor's injury. Imaging wasn't ready when I checked a few minutes ago, so I have no idea if the pins are ready to come out or not.

The minute I walk in the room, my eyes find Teagan. Her long hair is pulled up into a high ponytail, and the blue shirt she's wearing is the same shade of dress she wore on the riverboat tour.

Fuck. She's exquisite.

She's alone—which must mean Connor's still in imaging.

It takes everything in me not to sprint to her and take her in my arms. I've talked to her daily. But being on a small screen doesn't hold a candle to being in person. "Hey, how have you been?" I say casually since the door remains open for Connor and Miss Carol.

Her eyes go wide, and her mouth forms a perfect 'O' when she finds my gift for her.

Her eyes stay pinned to my chest as I reach up and adjust my tie.

The Tie.

The one I made all sorts of promises with last night.

Her face morphs from shocked to challenging as a sly grin spreads across her features. "You wore it."

"I told you I would."

"If all goes well today, Connor's being picked up by my mom after we get home. She's going to take him for an entire weekend. Don't take this the wrong way—but I hope we never have to see you again as his doctor."

"You and me both, T. Trust me."

I'd give anything to kiss her, but I force my feet to stay rooted in place.

Before either of us can say anything, there's a sound at the door. Miss Carol and Connor walk in the room, and I turn to face him. "Hey, Connor. It's great to see you again. Let's look at your arm and see if those pins are ready to come out."

Looking at me with those wide blue eyes that are replicas of his mother's, he nods profusely. "Yeah."

As Connor settles on the bench beside his mom, I pull out my ID to activate the computer. It only takes a minute to pull up his charts. Enlarging the image, I turn to Connor with a grin. "Guess what, Connor?"

"Am I all fixed?"

"Yep. We just need to take those pins out. You'll have to wear a bandage to keep them clean so they can heal."

His enthusiasm is infectious as he grins so wide, his face nearly splits in two. "Yay! Did you hear that, Mommy? I get my pins out."

"I sure did."

Then his expression turns from eager to hesitant as he bites on his lower lip, just like his mother when she's thinking. "Uh… will it hurt?"

"Not too bad. You'll just have to stay still for a few

minutes. There might be a little blood, so don't panic. That's what usually happens."

He nods in understanding, so I continue, "I will warn you though, you still need to take it easy with your arm for a bit. It might not move like you used to, but I'll send you to physical therapy and in a few weeks, you'll hardly know it's been broken."

His little brows knit together, and his lips pucker in the most adorable way as he looks from Teagan to me. "What's physical therapy?"

"Well, I'm a doctor who specializes in healing bones and ligaments in children. A physical therapist helps people like you who have been hurt, regain their ability to move. They'll have you do some exercises to strengthen your arm and make it so you're as good as new."

Connor nods in understanding. "My tummy feels bumpity. Can we get these out now?"

"Bumpity?" Looking to Teagan, I hope she'll fill me in.

"That means he's nervous."

"Ah, well... I can understand. Do you want to sit up here on the table, or with your mom?"

He looks to his mom and squeezes her hand. His voice is tiny when he says, "I just want it over."

"Let's get them out then."

Quickly reaching for a pair of gloves, I put them on while Miss Carol gets a bandage ready beside me.

Leaning on his mom, Teagan leans in and kisses his head. "Just close your eyes if you don't want to watch, Con. I'm right here."

Taking a deep breath, she reaches an arm around him, being careful to stay out of my way. The minute I reach for Connor's arm, I see his eyes close as well as hers. I work quickly to remove the pins and place them on the tray Miss Carol has ready for me. Taking a moment, I clean the wounds, then bandage them. The minute I have them covered, I announce to the room. "All done."

It melts my heart to hear both Connor and Teagan exhale heavily as one. Then Connor slowly opens his eyes, looks to his elbow, and winces as he tries to move it. "Ouch."

Bending down so I can get eye level with Connor, I pat him on his shoulder. "Sorry, buddy, it might hurt for a while. Your muscles have been stuck in that position for a long time, and it's kind of like putting them in the freezer. They're frozen stuck. I'll show you some exercises you can do when you feel up for it."

He nods in understanding, so I continue. "For the next week or so, if anything hurts too bad, just stop."

Nods come from each of them in understanding.

"You can start by making small movements. There will be some stiffness, so it might not be comfortable, but that's okay. But if there's a lot of pain, then listen to your body and stop."

Turning to Teagan, I ask, "Do you have a particular doctor you'd like, or can I refer you to one here at the outpatient clinic?"

"Here is fine."

"Well, then," I sigh, not quite ready for my time with her to end, "we're all set."

But there's no reason to prolong this appointment.

Normally, this is my cue to say it was great meeting them, and I remind them I'm here if they need anything in the future, but I can't bring myself to tell Connor I'll likely never see him again, when if I have it my way, this won't be the end.

"Thank you," Teagan says as she stands.

It's then I remember Connor's gift in my office, so I turn to Miss Carol. "I'll grab their discharge paperwork and be right back. I forgot something for Connor."

Miss Carol looks at me as if I'm crazy, but I don't care. Before anyone can say anything, I rush from the room. My office is on the other side of the clinic, so I'm breathless by the time I return.

The moment I return to the room, Connor's eyes light up as he jumps to his feet. "Chase!"

"I thought you might like him. He's been hanging out in my office, but I thought you might want to take him home with you. He's your favorite, right?"

Connor looks from me to his mom in surprise. "Can I?"

It's sweet how he asks his mom for permission.

She nods her approval, and Connor practically springs out of his shoes in my direction. The moment I hand it over, he hugs it with his good arm fiercely.

This is just one of the many reasons I love my job. Putting smiles back on patients' faces is priceless. Typically, I gift each of my younger children stuffed animals or toys, but usually, they're a generic stuffed animal to help them through their trauma.

Chase was bought especially for Connor, courtesy of my

one-click shopping. I have an entire set of the *Paw Patrol* cast at Derek's house, knowing they'll eventually all go to Connor.

"What do you say, Connor?"

"Thank you, Dr. Fallon. I love it!"

"Good. Now you take care of your mom and don't give her any more heart attacks and take it easy for a while."

Nodding profusely, Connor's grin is infectious. "M'kay."

To Teagan, I tilt my head. "Congratulations, Mom. We made it through this!"

Chapter 17
Teagan

THE MOMENT CONNOR leaves with my mom, I'm on pins and needles, waiting for Davis to arrive. He texts to say he's on his way, but I might wear a hole in my hardwood floors if he doesn't show up soon.

It's been over two months since we've been together and even though we've spoken each day for the last month, a part of me is waiting for the other shoe to drop. Apart from having to be apart so there won't be an ethics violation, he just feels too good to be true. What if we've built up all this hype but when we see each other regularly, it all fizzles out?

Even though I've been waiting for it, the minute the doorbell rings, I still jump out of my skin, as I've been stuck in my head for too long.

Rushing to the door, I fling it open so hard, it practically dents the wall.

His sexy grin and beautiful lips are all I can focus on. It was torture not kissing him or touching him in any way today. As if he can sense my need, he wordlessly closes the distance between us and crashes his glorious lips onto mine. Relief washes over me like rain after a never-ending drought. I've missed this man, and I need him more than I ever could have imagined.

There's no hesitation.

No awkwardness.

No holding back.

This kiss is everything we haven't been able to express these past months. My body clings to his like a magnet that's been held at bay and can no longer resist the current flowing between us.

I'm vaguely aware of moving inside the house and startle when the door slams shut.

Breaking our kiss, he pulls back with a smirk. "We're going to pretend that I didn't just smash the hell out of these flowers, and that I took you to dinner. We're going to pretend I had some restraint and didn't take you right against this wall."

A shiver flows through my body in anticipation.

Needing his lips back on mine, I smirk in agreement. "Yes, please."

His guttural moan makes every muscle in my body clench, and my pulse races. Through broken kisses, he makes my body his. "You taste... so fucking amazing, Teagan."

Kissing down my neck, his hands roam from my ass to my neck. With a firm grasp, he guides our kiss in the most devilish way, and I just can't get enough.

Heat pools in my panties, and I find myself grinding against his thigh in hopes of relieving the pressure. He smells as if he's fresh from the shower; his cologne is a tad stronger and more toxic to my senses than at the hospital earlier. With each inhale, I get drunk on all that is Davis.

God, I love this feeling.

"It's been way too long," he mutters as he kisses that soft spot behind my ear that drives me wild.

"Yes, it has," I pant out as he slides his hands along my thighs to my ass. I've never been more thankful for this skirt than in this moment.

Lifting me so that I'm straddling his waist, he growls, "Need you on a flat surface. Bedroom?"

As much as I don't want to break contact, the thought of all the things we can do to one another on a bed intrigues me. "Put me down, and we can get there faster." The moment my feet hit the floor, I reach for his hand and pull him past the kitchen into my bedroom.

Once inside my bedroom, I rip my blouse over my head. Sure, I'd taken the effort to put together a cute outfit, but I'd rather *it* spend the evening on my bedroom floor, than *I* spend another second without Davis.

When I turn to Davis, I find he'd stopped in the doorway to appreciate the view. I'm glad my little trip to the mall this week was worth it, by the look on his face. His eyes darken, and the devilish grin on his lips tells me he's plotting something I'm sure I'll thoroughly enjoy.

But I have plans of my own.

Shimmying out of my skirt, I maintain eye contact and feel emboldened when his breath stops as I let it pool on the floor at my feet. "You gonna join me, or is this gonna be a one-woman show tonight?"

"You look... beyond fucking words, Teagan. Your confidence..." He squeezes his eyes shut, then slowly, he reopens them. "Fuck—were you wearing those at the hospital today?"

Apparently, my bra and panty set are a score. It's totally out of my comfort zone, but when the sales lady suggested it, I tried it on. The black sheer lace cups do nothing to hide my nipples, but I loved the sexy geometric pattern. By the way his eyes linger, it makes them worth every cent I spent. I've paired it with satin geometric cut-out panties, which essentially leave my ass bare, but even I'll admit it's flattering and shows off my curves.

"Yep. I bought them especially for you."

"And it's not even my birthday. Hot damn. Turn around. Slowly. I have to see this entirely for myself."

As I turn, he slowly unbuttons his shirt, but the moment my backside comes into view, I hear him growl, and the shirt hits the floor. "I hope they had more of these, because I'll fucking buy you every color imaginable if it means I get to see you like this."

"You haven't even seen the best part," I tease as my belly flips in anticipation of him slowly stalking in my direction.

"Oh, yeah, what's that?" he asks when his lips are only inches from my ear.

A shiver runs through my spine, and my nipples harden to sharp points through the material. He must notice because he suddenly cups one breast and runs his thumb over the silky material, which elicits a moan to fall past my lips.

His voice is deep as he steals the words from my lips. "Fuck, that feels incredible."

"Hey, that's my line," I tease, reaching for the button of his jeans.

Running his fingertips lightly across the patterns of both my bra, then along the front of my panties as if he hadn't a care in the world, my body lights on fire. The satin is smooth, but his warm touch feels like a flame scorching its path as it leaves a trail from its wake. My spine tingles, and my muscles clench again from his simple touch.

Is it possible to come from his simple touch alone?

"What's the best part, Teagan?"

My name falling from his lips is a combination of sexy and sin as he leans in and licks his tongue along my neck and through the geometric cutouts of fabric. Fuck me. I feel his touch everywhere.

"Teagan?"

Shit. He's asked me a question. "You expect me to remember when you're doing that?"

When his hand slides up my inner thigh, I whisper, "You're about to find out."

The moment he comes into direct contact with my hot skin, he gasps. "You've got to be kidding me."

Then as if he's talking to himself more than me, he moans in the sexiest ways. "How will I ever concentrate knowing you could possibly be wearing these? Crotchless underwear—are you trying to kill me?"

"Nope—just wanted easy access to fuck you."

Reaching down, I cup his straining cock through his boxer briefs. "I've had a lot of time to fantasize about you these last few weeks. You're the one who opened the flood gates when you demanded I tell you what I want."

His sexy laugh fills the room as he dips a finger inside me and slides along my inner wall. "Really, what's that?"

Holy shit, I'm so wet and turned on, I can barely think.

In and out, he creates a rhythm that has my knees going weak and my head floating in the clouds. The moment his thumb presses against my clit, he circles it once, then stops.

Crying out in protest, I beg, "Don't stop."

Holding very still, he guides my head to look at him with his free hand at the base of my neck, until I can only look at him. "Then tell me what you want."

"Holy shit, you want me to form words?"

Sliding in and out once more, he flicks my clit in the perfect way.

Oh, God. That's incredible.

Then he stops, and I cry out.

Locking eyes with mine, his voice is low but demanding. "Tell me, or it stops."

Think, Teagan. Think. Give him words, so he'll keep stroking you.

"I've never been that adventurous." He starts the rhythm again.

His grin as he whispers has my core clenching, "I beg to differ, but go on."

"A... goal of mine is to be more adventurous... oh, right there. Don't stop."

"I won't, if you don't." He leans in and kisses the column of my neck.

Oh, that feels incredible.

"Hmmmm..... well, I want to wear a skirt like I was wearing tonight... do that again. I liked it... yeah, right there... I'll go somewhere with you in public. I'll wear these panties and ... oh, yes... grant you access... anytime you think you can get away with it."

"Access?" he asks, plucking a nipple into his mouth through the fabric and nipping on it in the most spectacular way.

Holy shit, I'm so close.

Never wanting him to stop, I continue, "Oh, God, Davis. You feel incredible... I want your fingers, cock, and anything you can think of to make me come... without... Oh my God, I'm so close... anyone knowing."

The moment I get my fantasy out, he presses down on my clit and guides my lips to meet his. My muscles lock up as a lightning bolt flashes behind my eyes. Waves of heat roll over me as my entire body convulses in pure pleasure.

"Holy shit, what are you doing to me?" That is my last coherent thought before I see stars, Somehow, he manages to hold my body upright because I feel as if my legs have turned to Jell-O, and I can barely stand on my own.

The next thing I know, I'm cradled in his arms, and he's carrying me to my bed as my body continues to pulse with aftershocks. Lying beside me, he brushes a hand through my hair and kisses me tenderly once more. Then he pulls back to just breathe with me.

No words need to be said, as I've never felt more

connected to any human in my entire life. Eventually, our breaths sync, and our pulses slow.

Reaching up to cup my face, he eventually whispers, "Hey, you."

Smiling at his cuteness, I run my fingers along his cheek. "Hey, yourself."

"I think I was supposed to have a bit more self-control, but the moment my lips touched yours, all thoughts of what I was supposed to do went out the window. Then... holy shit..." He sucks in a long breath before continuing, "Seeing you in this get-up turned into one of my dreams come true. You are so fucking sexy bundled up with a turtleneck or without a stitch of clothes on—It's you and your confidence that are my kryptonite, and I'm like a moth to a flame when it comes to needing you."

"Does that mean you think I'll be the death of you?" I tease.

Leaning in to kiss me once more, he grins. "Only in the best possible way. For the record, I want it all. I want to be a part of every fantasy you can conjure, and I'd love for you to be a part of mine."

"I think I can handle that. Can we start the next round with me on top?"

Laughter fills the room. "Oh, Teagan, you're insatiable—but please don't ever stop."

Chapter 18
Davis

FOR THE PAST WEEK, instead of our evening phone calls, I've been going to Teagan's after Connor falls asleep. Of course, I also leave each night at a decent time—especially if I have an early surgery. But I find myself wanting to squeeze out every possible moment with her.

I've invited her and Connor to spend the weekend with me at my grandparents' cabin before attending the Rainier Renegades game. But first, we discussed how to navigate our relationship with Connor; we've decided that I'd come over for dinner tonight, and we'll see how it goes from here.

I'll admit I'm nervous. But Teagan assures me it'll be okay even though I'm the first guy she's brought home to meet Connor. Hopefully, I won't fuck it up. I want to spend more time with her and get to know Connor better as well.

Walking up to their door, I wipe my sweaty palms against my jeans before ringing the bell. Taking in a deep breath, I remind myself that I can do this. I work with kids all the time, and I'll find a way to connect with him, too.

I hear the pitter-patter of feet approaching, and I'm certain he's going to beat Teagan to the door. "Hold up, Con. Let me help you open the door."

The minute it swings open, and Teagan's beautiful face appears, my racing heart is put at ease. Then I watch as Connor's face morphs from excitement to apprehension—and my nerves are back in full swing. What the fuck do I do now?

Forcing myself to use my words, I shrug. "Hi, Connor."

Looking from me to his mom, his features fill with guilt. "Are you... here to put my cast back on? I only jumped from the back porch one time. I bumped my arm. It doesn't hurt. I promise." He sputters it out in practically one sentence as if he's somehow giving a confessional.

His cuteness is just what I need to relieve my tension, and I can't help but laugh at his logic. "No. I'm not here to put your cast back on. I've come for dinner. Your mom says you've helped make a mean casserole and invited me over. Is that okay with you?"

"And I won't have to get another surgery?"

"Oh, sweet boy, no," Teagan insists as she pulls him into a side hug. "Davis is a friend of mine, and I invited him to dinner."

"Okay, but can we have ice cream for dessert?" And just like that, he runs into the house and leaves Teagan and me at the door.

Leaning in, I give her a chaste kiss, then follow her into the house.

Teagan's house has an open floor plan and as I follow them into the kitchen, Connor rushes to the counter where he has a stool he can stand on to help. "Is it ready yet? I'm hungry."

"Just about. Want to wash your hands and set the table?"

Before he leaves, he turns to me and asks, "Wanna see where Chase sleeps? I've been takin' good care of him."

His mother pipes in before I can answer, "How about we show him *after* dinner? It's ready, and I don't want it to get cold."

His body droops like a wilted flower, but he says, "Okay. Be right back."

Turning to Teagan, I ask, "Need help with anything?"

"Nope. It's ready. Mind if we watch a show tonight? I promised Connor if he took a bath earlier, he could stay up and watch a show."

"I think I can handle that."

Connor rushes back into the room and quickly puts the three plates Teagan had set out onto the table. Then he zips to the silverware drawer and pulls out three forks. He's still favoring his arm and keeps it in the position it was in from the cast, but it's extended further than he could at our last visit, so that's progress.

When he's done he looks to me and asks, "You sit here next to me. M'kay?"

"Of course." Taking my assigned seat, he offers a toothy grin, and my heart squeezes.

So far so good.

When he climbs into the chair beside me, he asks with the most serious expression, "Did you know humans are the only animals with chins?"

Okay. That's random but adorable, and I can't help but

smile. "I believe I heard that before. But do you know that your nose and ears never stop growing?"

Instantly, his eyes go wide as he reaches for his ear and tugs it. "Really? Like never? Will it grow bigger than my face?"

Oh my, this kid will keep me on my toes. "Naw. It will stay in proportion to your face, I'm sure. At least, I've never seen anyone but the BFG have giant ears—but he's a fictional giant after all."

His blank expression tells me he doesn't have a clue, and I've clearly gone over his head. Quickly, I explain, "It was one of my favorite books growing up."

Nodding, he understands. "I love it when Mommy reads me books. I love learning about facts and when she does voices for stories."

"Your mom's pretty special," I admit.

"Yep. She even says she has eyes in the back of her head. But I haven't seen them, so I think she's just teasin'."

Teagan's beautiful laugh fills the room as she pretends to look stern. "I'll never tell."

"My mom always knew everything we did growing up, too. I think it's their super power."

"Can your mom tell when you haven't brushed your teeth?"

Teagan's smile is wide as she brings the casserole to the table.

"Yep. They always know. It's best to do it and get it over with. My mom could also tell which one of the kids took showers, too."

Suddenly, he looks me over from head to toe in disbelief. "You didn't like showers?"

"At your age—maybe. But now I love them."

"Okay, boys. Let's dish up and start eating—or we won't get to watch a movie before bed."

About thirty minutes later, the kitchen is clean, and we're settling on the couch. Once again, Connor insists on sitting next to me. Well, between Teagan and myself. As time has passed, my nerves settle, and I've relaxed. Even though this is entirely out of my wheelhouse, being with them just feels right.

We've settled in to watch *Encanto*. Apparently, this is a new favorite of Connor's, and I can see why. Even as an adult, I'm pulled in from the start. But what makes the movie for me is when Connor and Teagan sing along with the lyrics. Connor wiggles his body between us along to the music.

It's so endearing, I wish the music would never stop. They're adorable together and have many of the same traits. Expressive eyes, beautiful smiles, and sing in complete abandon as if they're the ones putting on the show at times.

And I can't get enough.

Eventually, he settles into my side. To give him more room, I rest my arm on the back of the couch. Not only does it allow him to settle further, but my fingers can run through the hair at the back of Teagan's neck. Even a simple touch as this excites me, yet somehow grounds me at the same time. Even though this is entirely new for me, it somehow just feels right.

After about an hour, Connor's no longer talking, and his body feels heavy against me. Looking down, I see he's conked out. His little lips are upturned into a smile, and he looks almost angelic. I'm startled when he stretches in his sleep and throws an arm around me as if he's hugging me.

"Sorry about that," Teagan whispers. "Want me to move him? We don't have to watch the end of the movie."

"Uh... yes, we do. I need to find out why they don't talk about Bruno. We've gotten this far, I'm invested. So, hush up and let's finish this show."

Teagan's light laugh is beautiful to hear. "But what about Con? Need me to move him?"

"Absolutely not. Though I wouldn't complain if you moved to the other side of me, so I can hold your hand."

Her couch is a sectional, therefore there's plenty of room.

Patting the place beside me, I waggle my brows. "What do you say, T? Can I hold your hand?"

Rolling her eyes, she grins playfully but sighs heavily, "If I must." Then her voice changes to a whisper as she almost mutters, "If you don't watch out, I might just catch feelings for you." But she stands and settles into my other side.

Leaning in, I kiss her chastely on the lips. "That's kinda the point."

Her mouth drops open, but before she can say anything, I nod toward the TV and playfully remind her, "Shhh... We're about to learn about Bruno."

Chapter 19

Davis

IT TAKES A LITTLE CONVINCING, but I somehow manage to get Teagan to agree to come with me to my grandparents' house on Anderson Island for the entire weekend before the game. Selfishly, I want to spend an entire night with her, without making it awkward for me to be there in the morning with Connor. I'm dying to have her wake up in my arms.

With Derek and Tessa coming back for the game, I also feel weird coming in late at night now that they have Melody. Since my family's cabin is free for the weekend, it's a win for all. The plan is to spend the weekend on the island, then leave from there for the Renegades game on Sunday.

Even though it's a short ferry ride to Anderson Island, Connor is excited to get out and walk on top of the ferry. It's a beautiful Friday afternoon. Typically, there's a lot of rain in early November, but today, it's clear and nearly fifty degrees. We can't ask for better weather in Washington.

When we get to the top of the stairs from the car deck, I'm shocked when Connor reaches for my hand and pulls me to the outside deck. "Come on, Davis. Let's go out there."

To him, it's a simple gesture. He just reaches up as if he's been doing this his entire life and drags me outside.

For me, it's a moment I'm sure I'll remember forever.

We've spent a lot of time together this week, but he's never just reached for my hand. My chest tightens as a grin follows him eagerly. Teagan is a few steps behind us, and I look to her to make sure she's following. Instead of being right behind us, she's stopped as if frozen in place with her hand covering her heart.

Holy shit, have I done something wrong?

Then I dart my eyes to her face, and I see the grin spreading from ear to ear, and my heart resumes its normal beat.

Before I can say anything, Connor points out. "Is that the island?"

"Yep. My grandparents have had a place here for as long as I can remember. I used to spend a lot of time here in the summers."

"Is the water warm? Can we go swimming?" His eyes plead.

"It's freezing—especially this time of year. If you want to swim, we'll go to an indoor pool sometime," Teagan suggests.

Connor looks hopefully to me. "Can Davis come?"

Warmth spreads throughout my body over the fact that he's included me. "I can make that happen."

Even though I try to keep public displays of affection to a minimum around Connor, when Teagan steps closer, I find myself wrapping an arm around her instinctively. As time has gone on, I thought my feelings for her might wane, but I've quickly learned they just keep growing stronger.

By the time we make it to my family's home on the island, Connor's turned into a chatter box. He's asked just about any question he can think of under the sun. There's not much daylight left, so I suggest we bring our things into the cabin, then go for a walk along the shore of the Puget Sound near the house.

However, the moment we get outside and Connor sees the expansive playground my brothers have put in the backyard, that plan disappears. "Can I play on that?"

"Sure." I smile with delight as I watch him run up to the tower, leading to the slide.

"Wow. You didn't tell me your family had their own park."

Shaking my head, I laugh at the memory. "It wasn't always this way, trust me. But between Dani and Damien's kids, the old rope swing just wasn't enough." I point to the original swing that used to entertain us for hours. "Though Jules wouldn't let us take it away. I'll never forget the look on her face when she came to visit once this monstrosity of a play structure was complete."

There are four swings hanging from twelve-foot posts in the middle, a tall straight slide, and a twisty slide coming from both ends they have to climb either a series of platforms or a rock wall to get to. "When Jules started gymnastics, she asked for a bar to twirl on. Before I knew it, my dad had put one in for her. When we were kids, we spent our days exploring the woods next door, but Mom wanted to be able to see her grandbabies play, and with Damien being an engineer, he went a little overboard."

"I think it's great."

"Look at me, Davis," Connor says from the top of the twisty slide as he jumps inside it. "Wheee."

Teagan slides up beside me and hip-checks me as she tucks her arms around herself just as a gust of wind picks up. "I think you have a fan."

"I think it's the other way around. He's an amazing human being, and I love spending time with him. Thank you for letting me be a part of his life."

Teagan's quiet for a moment, then slowly turns to me.

My heart crashes into my chest when I see unshed tears forming in her eyes.

Shit. What's wrong now?

Replaying my words, I still can't figure out what I've said to make her react this way. Reaching for her cheek, I brush a tear away with my thumb. "Hey, what's wrong?"

"Nothing," she says through a smile.

"It's not nothing, or you wouldn't be crying. What's really wrong?"

Teagan reaches up to caress my face, and warmth spreads throughout my body. "Nothing. Absolutely nothing. I just love that you view him as a gift."

My throat feels tight when I admit, "He is... and so are you. I'm falling in love with you both and for the first time in my life—everything feels complete."

Her eyes widen, and her jaw drops then she sputters, "But... but we just... met."

Leaning in, I press a finger to her lips. "It's okay if you're not there yet. You don't have to say anything."

For a long moment, we just stare at one another. Then I lean in and kiss her tenderly to show her just how serious I am. When I pull back, we're both breathless.

Locking eyes with her, I get lost in their beauty and right then and there, everything clicks into place, and I throw down a challenge I'll keep for the rest of my life.

"But fair warning—You're it for me."

Epilogue

Teagan

Two Years Later

AS I WALK OUT of Davis's family's house on Anderson Island carrying a birthday cake, I realize he's made good on that promise. It wasn't even four months later, and he proposed to me right here in this very yard in front of his entire family and mine.

Of course, he'd brought me here under the guise of a family barbecue. He'd invited my parents so they could finally meet his, and I had no clue a proposal was coming. He had planned everything perfectly. He even involved Connor as well as members of his family. He'd never admit it, but I'm sure his sister Dani had something to do with it, too.

Connor and I quickly bonded with his siblings and their families during that first Rainier Renegades game we attended. We've been getting together about once a month to let the kids play and spend time with one another. They're ecstatic that Davis is back in Washington and want to make up for lost time.

That time, we'd decided to all meet up at the Island since Luke was done with his season and their grandparents were back from their trip to Arizona. I'd been over at Dani's, helping her do something for her website, while Davis and Luke brought the kids over here to play with everyone.

Eventually, he'd called to say dinner was ready, so we returned to eat with the family.

When I walked into the backyard, everyone including the kids had gone silent. Which was weird. The Fallon family is big and loud and *never* quiet. Then I spotted Davis and Connor standing at the far edge of the yard. Without a word, his entire family formed two long lines in the yard. Each of them had knowing smiles, and some had things in their hands.

Reaching for my hand, Dani squeezed it to get my attention. "Um... Davis asked me to give you this." She handed me a piece of paper. Confused, I took it and immediately knew what was happening. It was a postcard. On the front was a picture of Tilly's, the B&B where we met.

Dani whispered, "There's a message on the back. Make sure you read it aloud."

Sure enough, in Davis's handwriting, there was a message:

I started out as your stalker.

Grinning, I'd turned to Davis, but Dani had ushered me to their mom Daisy, who handed me another card to read.

This time, it was a picture of us together on the riverboat tour.

What were the odds we'd be on the same tour?

The next photo had come from his brother Derek. It was a picture of the children's hospital in Austin.

Or that you'd trust me enough to help Connor?

Derek's wife, Tessa, handed me the next postcard. I had nearly choked on my own spit at the picture of Davis standing next to a giant rooster sculpture.

I come with a giant … Rooster. (Yes - pun intended)

And sure enough, Luke stepped up with a multicolored sculpture of a giant rooster in his hands. By now, tears streamed down my cheeks from both anticipation of what was to come and his audacity. Oh my God, that man has always made me laugh—thank God his family has a great sense of humor.

Next was a card from Damien. It was a postcard of his family from our first Renegades game. Everyone except his parents and grandparents were in the photo. It had been taken at dinner that evening.

And an invasive family—who will have your back until the end of time.

Then my dad came up and handed me a picture of my mom, dad, Davis, and Connor from the first time Davis had come to meet them.

We give you our love and blessing.

Last was a card from my sweet boy. He walked up as confident as ever and reached for my hand to walk me to Davis. When we were only a few feet away, he put his card into my hand and said, "I love you, Mommy... and Davis, too." His card slayed me.

It was a picture of the three of us.

This time, it was written in Connor's handwriting.

I'm ready if you are.

PS—can I have a puppy?

Then he placed another one in my hand as he said, "Mine didn't fit on one card, so you get two."

Or maybe a little brother?

Then my little man walked me to Davis. Before he let go of my hand, he turned me to him and said, "Can we marry Davis?"

When I returned my attention to Davis, he'd been on one knee with a ring in his hand. "What do you say, Teagan? Will you be my wife, so Connor can be my son?"

Of course, I'd been a blubbering mess by that point and said something I don't recall, as I'd jumped into his arms and gave him my answer.

"Teagan, need help with that?" Daisy breaks me from my trip down memory lane.

Shaking my head, I quickly tell her, "No. I've got this. But can you help Cameron get into the high chair so we can sing to her? Davis is helping Connor grab the plates."

Cameron has been our best surprise yet. Davis had convinced me to ditch birth control pills the moment we were married, so we could work on getting Connor his requested sibling. The moment we found out I was pregnant, I couldn't contain Davis's excitement. I swear, if he could have, he would've rented a giant jumbotron or took out an ad on national TV. He was so excited to become a father. What's funny is he knew I was pregnant first, so I didn't even have to go through the process of telling him. Apparently, my boobs had grown and I was a bit emotional, so he made me take a test.

It's been so much different having a partner to help me with my pregnancy and newborn stage. I'm sure Jacob would've been a great dad, but he never got that opportunity. Davis has been here every step of the way, and I can't help but love him more each day. Not only did he adopt Connor when we married later that summer, to make him his, but his daughter has him wrapped around her little finger, too.

Setting the cake on the table we'd set up outside, I feel two strong arms snake around me. "It's hard to believe our baby turns one next week."

Spinning around in his arms, I loop mine around his neck.

"I know, and next year, we'll have three kids under the age of six."

He runs a hand over my stomach. We haven't told anyone yet as I'm forcing him to wait until I'm twelve weeks along, but I can already tell that might be a huge feat for him as he's so excited to add to our family.

Leaning in, he whispers into my ear so only I can hear, "Admit it, Teagan, you love my magical cock. We make eggselent babies."

Oh my God, I can't even with this man.

"Don't worry, Davis, I love you in spite of your horrible dad jokes!"

"Teagan, my dear. I'm a proud dad of three. Don't worry—like wine, they'll just get better with age."

Before I can say anything, he plants a toe-curling kiss on my lips.

He's right. We do get better with age.

The End

THANK you for reading **He Saved My Boy**. If you've enjoyed this book, I'd be honored if you'd leave a review on your favorite retailer. There are so many books you can choose to read, so thank you for taking the time to read mine.

· · ·

IF YOU WANT MORE from the Fallon family, you'll be happy to know that each sibling has a book of their own in **Making the Call**, **Damien**, and **The Boy Upstairs**. If you're not ready for your time with them to end, don't worry; neither am I.

Annie and Nate are featured in **The Vegas Pitch** and as her best friend, Teagan and Davis are a part of their story as well.

AS ALWAYS, if you want to learn more about my books, please visit my website at www.amandashelley.com to learn more. So that you don't miss out on any upcoming book, feel free to join my newsletter today. https://geni.us/AmandaShelleyNL

KEEP READING to find out more books by Amanda Shelley

ACKNOWLEDGMENTS

First, I would like to thank you the reader, blogger, and reviewer for taking the time to read this book. I'd love to hear from you and your thoughts about Davis and Teagan. You can find me on social media, my reader's group *Amanda's Army of Readers*, or at www.amandashelley.com. If you care to share your thoughts on this book with other book lovers, please consider leaving a review at any of the retail sites or on Goodreads, BingeBooks, and BookBub.

Next, I'd like to thank Sierra Hill for putting together the All American Boy Series and allowing me to continue to participate again. It was so much fun to work with such amazing authors and create this world. What a great way to collaborate personally and professionally. Thank you so much for this experience.

This book wouldn't be what it is without my amazing team of support. To Renita McKinney at A Book A Day Author Services, thank you for helping me develop Davis's and Teagan's characters and make them into the best they can be. Thanks also for helping me grow and develop as an author as well. I appreciate your bluntness and for always giving me the push I need.

To Susan Soares at SJS Editorial Services, thank you for

working with me. This book wouldn't be what it is today without you. I appreciate your time and feedback. You're amazing to work with, and I appreciate that you've been with me since the beginning. You are the best.

To Julie Deaton at Deaton Author Services, thanks for making my book pretty. I appreciate knowing your proofreading is exquisite, and my worries disappear. Your eagle eyes are spectacular, and I don't know what I'd do without you. Your reactions to my books are priceless.

To the people who have supported me along the way, I'm humbly grateful to have you in my life. Whether you've read my books, asked me about my progress, listened to me talk about my fictional characters as if they're a part of my family, plotted with me, or been my cheerleader, I appreciate your continued support. Please know it hasn't gone unnoticed.

Last, but certainly not least, to my four beautiful girls who have had to wait patiently when I said, "Just one more minute," when I obviously meant a lot more than one. I love that you get that I have deadlines and will sometimes keep me on task with your not-so-subtle reminders that "Mom... you should be working," during my designated times. I appreciate your support more than you'll ever know. Even though you can't read these books—because that might be *weird*—for both of us, I love that you keep asking. I love you all more than words can express. You're the reason I continue to strive and reach for my goals each day.

If you enjoyed this book, you will be happy to discover Amanda Shelley primarily writes in one world. For a complete list of the series reading order as well as a chronological time line, please visit:

https://amandashelley.com/reading-order/

Making The Call

Dani

As a bestselling romance author, most assume my life's glamorous, filled with combustible chemistry, and most of all, romance. Ha! I can only wish. With a deadline looming, I've escaped to my family's cabin on Anderson Island to free myself from distractions. My plan's great, until a man, who could pass as a cover model on one of my books, comes to my rescue. Is there chemistry? Sure. Is he everything I'd look for in a guy? Absolutely. But will my career be at risk if I give into my desire?

Luke

For a player, women line up outside the locker room. For coaches, we're lucky to get in the game. As the youngest NFL coach in the league, I live, eat, breathe, and even sleep football. To gear up for this season, I return to my home on Anderson Island for a much-needed break. When Dani literally crashes into my life, my mind's suddenly on the sexy brunette with a sailors mouth, rather than my team's next play. She has me dusting off another playbook entirely, making me wonder, did I make the right call?

https://geni.us/AmandaShelleyBooks

The Vegas Pitch

This pitch could make or break my career.

Not only will it set a personal record for the biggest account I've ever landed, but it could set my newfound company three years ahead of schedule for expansion.

Thank god I've got Nate Bellinger on my team.

Even though I had my reservations hiring the sexiest man I've ever laid eyes on – he more than meets my expectations with his hard work and determination. Together, we've formed a solid team and play off each other perfectly.

As we wait for the final verdict, I begrudgingly take Nate up on his offer for a night on the town. After all, this is Vegas and I need to let the chips fall where they may.

Imagine my surprise when I wake up the next morning to find we've not only won the campaign, but I'm apparently married to the man I've only ever let myself fantasize about.

The kicker of it all – he has no intentions of letting me go.

But what will it mean once we leave Vegas?

https://geni.us/AmandaShelleyBooks

Zander: A Perfectly Independent Series Novella

Zander's known for being a player both on and off the court. When his name shows up as my next client, my heart stalls, and not in a good way. There's no way I'll survive the semester with him. I just don't have the patience.

However, when I need help, Zander makes a proposal I can't refuse. He'll be my fake date to my best friend's wedding so I don't have to face my ex and his new girlfriend alone.

The weekend goes off without a hitch as we effortlessly pretend to have the time of our lives.

All is perfect... until I realize my feelings for Zander are no longer an act.

What will I do when our arrangement comes to an end?

https://geni.us/AmandaShelleyBooks

Drew: Book One of the Perfectly Independent Series

Of all people, why him?

He didn't EVEN bother introducing himself, just assumed I knew him from his fame on the court.

I nearly died on the spot when our professor announced we were permanent lab partners. Between his arrogance and the constant interruption from basketball groupies, there's no way I'll survive this semester.

Sure, he's hotter than anyone I've ever seen in a science lab with his sexy blue eyes, cute dimple, and muscles for days - but I can't afford *his* kind of distractions.

Okay. Deep breath.

I can do this.

After all, it's only one semester.

Just when I think my self-control is in check, he does something to show me that he isn't the egotistical, self-centered jerk I thought he was.

How can his stupid smile suddenly make my mind melt, heart race, and palms sweat?

If I take this chance on Drew, will my perfectly laid out plans disappear?

https://geni.us/AmandaShelleyBooks

Vince: Book Two of the Perfectly Independent Series

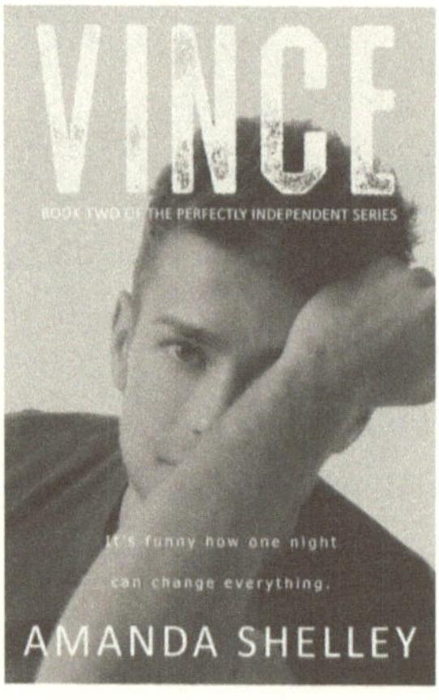

It's funny how one night can change everything.

As a bartender near campus, I'm certain I've heard it all. Rarely a shift passes without some guy taking his best shot, hoping I'll end my self-proclaimed dating diet.

Of course, this is exactly how I meet Vince.

Except, he isn't the one running his mouth.

No, he simply shuts down his idiotic friend, then stops my heart with the simplest of smiles and walks away.

Just when I force myself to forget him, he bumps into me on campus.

Our connection is consuming, and my world is knocked off kilter. It's far beyond physical attraction. He's smart, sexy, and feels like—home?

Wait, that can't be right...

Whatever it is, Vince has me breaking my rules to spend time with him.

My entire life I've prepared for meeting the wrong guys.

What the hell should I do when I find the right one?

https://geni.us/AmandaShelleyBooks

Damien: Book Three of the Perfectly Independent Series

Beautiful girls are not hard to find at Columbia River University.

The coeds on campus are great to look at but I was over that scene after graduation three years ago.

These days, outside of being part of the largest civil engineering job on campus, all I'm searching for is a decent meal and some peace and quiet. It's why I'm happy to have found what I consider a hidden gem in the diner I frequent.

All I need to do is finish this job and move on to the next by year's end.

Should be easy enough. Only when Vanessa walks up with a sexy smile and a mouth full of sass, she does more than take my order. She completely takes my breath away.

Next thing I know, I'm here every morning, making every excuse to dine with this intriguing woman. Not only is she smart and sexy, but she's laser focused on reaching the goals she's set for herself.

The more I get to know her, the more I'm convinced she's the one. I just have to find a way to get her to deviate from her perfectly laid plans and take a chance on me.

https://geni.us/AmandaShelleyBooks

The Summer Dare

Leave it to Nana to think of everything.

After a grueling semester, I'm ready for a peaceful summer in Seaside with my sisters.

Imagine my surprise, when I'm woken by the screeching sound of a saw coming through my wall, the first official morning of break.

Not only did I come flying out of bed swinging, but I gave Ryan, the unsuspecting carpenter the surprise of his life, when I came wielding my killer coat hanger and all.

Too bad, I was only in a tank and undies and it wasn't nearly as effective as I'd hoped.

Of course, he insists he's only doing his job. Since it's Nana's last request to care for us, I can't refuse.

However, I won't let a tall, pesky, sexy as sin, know-it-all get in my way of my summer plans. I pretend I ignore him – that is until my youngest sister pokes her nose in my business and throws down a dare I can't back down from.

Kiss the next single guy who walks up to the bonfire – or explain to my sisters why I get riled up over the contractor.

When Ryan suddenly appears, I know I'm screwed in more ways than one.

Not only will my sisters learn my secret, but from the determined look on Ryan's face, I'm afraid he's eager to reveal it to the world as well.

What have I gotten myself into?

As I walk toward him, one thing is certain – this summer dare will either make or break me.

https://geni.us/AmandaShelleyBooks

The Summer Ultimatum

Watching my sister fall in love last summer gave me something I hadn't expected—hope. It gave me hope that there might be someone out there for me and hope that I might get past my misguided fears and finally let someone in.

With my help, Ryan's planning the most epic proposal. I just have to get the know-it-all musician I work with to fall in line to make it work.

Jax is wicked smart, extremely talented, and sexy as sin. But he can't see the forest for the trees when it comes to his potential. He'd rather keep playing in dive bars along the coast than take a real shot at success.

When the Seaside festival has a music competition, I present Jax with an ultimatum that will either make or break both our careers.

I've laid it all on the line, but can he?

https://geni.us/AmandaShelleyBooks

The Summer Proposal

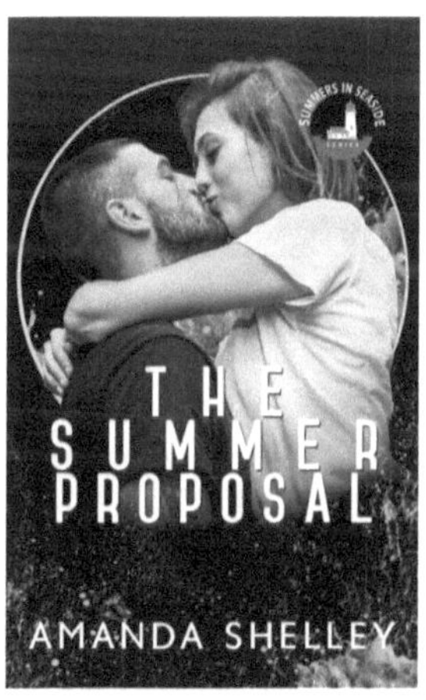

My sisters are dropping like flies.

They're falling in love and having the time of their lives.

Don't get me wrong, I'm ecstatic for them. I love seeing them happy.

But I'm not ready for that type of commitment.

I can't even keep a plant alive, let alone find someone worthy of getting past a third date.

As the only sister done with school and single as a pringle, I have to do something fast, or I'll be my matchmaking aunt's next victim.

When Jax's drummer joins him for the summer and needs some help with his image, I make him a deal he can't refuse.

All is perfect—until I realize my summer proposal has one minor flaw.

Our relationship may be a sham, but there's nothing fake about my feelings for Finn.

https://geni.us/AmandaShelleyBooks

The Summer Arrangement

One, two, three—it's all down to me.

As the youngest and only single Lancaster, I'm eager to spend my summer in Seaside, Oregon, with my sisters. It's something I've looked forward to all year, and I'm determined to make every minute count. After all, I've only got one year before I graduate from college and have to adult for real.

However, if I want to graduate debt free, I need to work. I have a lead on the perfect summer job with the nanny agency I've spent the last three summers catering to.

I just have to win over an adorable three-year-old and convince her single dad I'm the right one for the job.

Simple enough, right?

Except when I show up at his door, I'm shocked to find he's the guy I hooked up with a few times last semester.

This cannot be happening.

I need this job. There's too much on the line to walk away. Maybe we can put the past behind us and make some sort of summer arrangement?

https://geni.us/AmandaShelleyBooks

The Summer I Found Home

Being a pilot is all I've ever known.

I served my country and I'm damn proud of my career.

But sacrifices were made, especially when it came to family.

I've missed first steps, first days of school, and first dates to name a few.

My kids grew up. They're having families of their own.

Was it worth it?

When an opportunity brings me to Seaside, I jump feet first no questions asked.

It means experiencing all those firsts with my grandkids.

With family as my focus and my guard down, I don't even see Faye coming.

She's a force to be reckoned with and has me holding on for dear life.

I thought our ship had sailed, but now that I'm home for good—I just might get more than one second chance.

arrangement?

Resilience: Book One of Resilience Duet

Resolution: Book Two of Resilience Duet

Samantha never saw Enzo coming.

As the dust settles from her divorce, her life is full. She doesn't have time for distractions. She's too busy running her own company and checking off numerous items from her kids' demanding schedule to have a life of her own.

Then he walks into her kitchen with his breathtaking green eyes and a mischievous grin. He's there to surprise his father - her contractor, but his presence makes everything off kilter.

Enzo's perfectly content with his adventurous life as an elite rescue pilot, until a harmless prank turns on him. Instead of surprising his father, he finds his world thrown off course by the beautiful woman with a sexy smile, wicked sass and the mouthwatering ability to keep him on his toes.

With his limited time on leave, is she worth the risk to his heart?

https://geni.us/AmandaShelleyBooks

Collide: A Sweet Romance

Falling head over heels was the last thing I expected.

Literally.

Coffee is everywhere – and more than my ego is bruised.

When the handsome stranger I plowed into calls me by name, mortification sinks in.

He rushes off to class. I run home to change, hoping to forget the whole incident.

If only I could be so lucky.

I quickly find it's a small world and Gavin Wallace is completely unavoidable. Everywhere I turn he's there. In my classes. Hanging with my friends.

I've got his full attention and I have to admit, I like it a lot more than I should.

https://geni.us/AmandaShelleyBooks

ABOUT AMANDA SHELLEY

Amanda Shelley writes romantic stories you can escape into. Some are steamy, others are sweet but all have strong characters with a little bit of sass.

When not writing, Amanda enjoys time with her family, playing chauffeur, chef and being an enthusiastic fan for her children. Keeping up with them keeps her alert and grounded in reality. She enjoys long car rides, chai lattes and popping her SUV into four-wheel drive for adventures anywhere.

Amanda loves hearing from readers. Be sure to sign up for her newsletter and follow her on social media. Join her reader's group Amanda's Army of Readers to stay up to date on her latest information.

Readers group: https://www.facebook.com/groups/Amandas
ArmyofReaders/
Goodreads: https://www.goodreads.com/author/show/
19713563.Amanda_Shelley
Newsletter: https://geni.us/AmandaShelleyNL
www.amandashelley.com